THE

FALLEN

BODY

BY STONE PATRICK

To order additional copies of this book, contact:

Tayman International Ventures LLC

www.taylorsbookpub.com

taylor.stonely@gmail.com

Chapter 1

Why is a total stranger wearing my dead mother's watch?

The lady wearing it was of average height and thin, in her late 30's, and she had just finished putting her groceries in her black SUV. She brushed aside her hair from her fine-featured face, which reminded Taylour of a Greek marble statue.

"Where'd you get that watch?"

"Sorry?"

"That watch. It's a Kenneth Cole, right?"

The owner of the SUV looked Taylour over and saw a woman slightly younger than herself, with strawberry blonde hair and an inquisitive look on her face, her green eyes looking straight at her. She cocked her head to one side. "This was given to me by my husband on our 1st anniversary. Do I know you?" She fingered the watch with her right hand and moved it back and forth around her delicate wrist.

"That same watch was on my mom's wrist when we buried her three years ago. I remember because it seemed like such a waste to have such a beautiful piece go into the ground." Tears welled up, but Taylour forced the memory away. It was hard to stop the heartache, but she managed. "My brother insisted, though, and I really couldn't say otherwise since he was the one who gave it to her."

"I'm sorry about your mom."

Sniffing, Taylour stuck out her hand, "I'm Taylour Dixxon. Sorry, I didn't mean to trouble you as you are obviously in a hurry."

She took her hand, grinned at Taylour, and said, "That's OK. I'm new in town and don't know anyone really. My name's Sarah."

"Are you the ones who bought the old Wharton place, on Oak Avenue?"

"Well, I inherited it. I live by myself now. No kids." Sarah glanced at her watch, took a sharp breath, and said, "Sorry, gotta go. I have a conference call I need to be on in ten minutes and I really need to get these groceries in before they melt."

"Well, it was nice meeting you, Sarah." Taylour wondered if she would see Sarah again, not realizing that their chance encounter in the ALDI's parking lot was just the beginning.

* * *

Later that same evening, Taylour sat on the porch, sipping some raspberry lemonade, when a black SUV pulled up. It appeared to be the same vehicle that she saw Sarah drive away in earlier. Sure enough, there she was again, on the phone. She stepped out of her vehicle and closed her cell phone after finishing her call.

Taylour stood up, almost spilling her lemonade on her pants in her haste, and said, "Welcome!"

"Taylour, I hope you don't mind me dropping by unannounced like this. I asked around to find out where you lived, because I had to talk with you. Something you said earlier struck me as familiar, and I had to find out if I was right."

Taylour replayed their previous conversation in her head, but came up empty. "Happy to help. Would you like some lemonade?"

"No thanks, I won't be long. I wanted to, er... ask a question about your mother."

Taylour motioned for Sarah to sit on the wicker chair next to hers. Sarah sat on the edge, back straight as a board, and said, "I knew your mother."

Taylour's eyes got big, but she said nothing.

"At least, I think I knew your mother. Her name was Doris Dixxon, right?"

Taylour raised her eyebrows and nodded. "She went by her middle name, which was Victoria, but yeah, that was her name."

"Well, I knew of her because my younger sister was her oncology nurse at St. John's Hospital, and she told me about this lady who always wore her Kenneth Cole watch whenever she came in for her radiation treatments. It only stood out in her mind because it was exactly like my watch. Here, take a look." She pulled off the time piece and handed it to Taylour.

It was gunmetal gray, with ceramic links that were warm on the underside, but cool on the outside. There was a fold-over, two button clasp that snapped in place, and two sub-dials on the classic round mother of pearl face, which was clean and without any visible scratches. Taylour turned it over and noticed that it was inscribed with a date and a personal sentiment. She squinted and held it closer. It said, "June 12, 2005 - May Time Never Stop On Our Love For Each Other."

Chuckling, she handed it back to Sarah, who gave Taylour a blank stare. Taylour fidgeted in her seat and said, "That seems a bit ironic, don't you think? You are single, right?"

Sarah sighed and turned her head. She looked like she wanted to say something, but she didn't. Finally, she looked Taylour in the eyes. "Will you please tell me about your mother and how she died?"

Taylour relaxed her posture. "She died of cancer, as you already know. Lung cancer. Didn't get diagnosed until she was at Stage IV. By then the doctors didn't want to operate on her since it had spread, so they tried radiation and chemotherapy. She was at St. John's for the radiation treatments, which was probably when she met your sister. What was her name?"

"Melanie Woods."

"Is your last name Woods as well?"

Sarah blushed, "I'm sorry, I didn't ever tell you my last name. It's Cockrell."

"Nice to meet you, Sarah Cockrell." Taylour swept her left arm up and said, "Welcome to Dixxon Manor, the prettiest place this side of the Brazos River." Taylour took a deep breath through her nose, taking in the aroma of the crisp autumn air. "This is where I grew up. I was the only one in my family that stuck around, so when my mom died, I got the house. My dad passed away several years ago, and my brother lives in Dallas with his wife and kids."

"I bet that's nice, having family only a few hours away."

Taylour dropped her eyes, "Well, I'm awful busy, and so are they, so we really only see each other once or twice a year, usually around Thanksgiving. I've got my law practice that keeps me from going crazy from boredom."

"Oh, you're a lawyer?"

The Fallen Body

"Yep, mostly land contracts, estate planning, the occasional DUI. Nothing major. Kinda nice to not have too much going on around here."

"My dad was a police officer in Trenton, just retired last year after thirty years. He hates lawyers."

Taylour smirked. "Do you?"

Sarah squirmed in her chair, the creaking audible. "I guess that I have never had much use for them."

"Yeah, most people don't need us until they do. It's a noble profession, and I can handle the jokes thrown my way." Taylour leaned forward and placed her glass on the floorboard. "What I can't stand are the clients that dismiss what I do for them, as if they could do it themselves. Most don't have a clue what's involved. And being a woman. Pfft!" Taylour shrugged and said, "I'm not some feminist or anything, but I do like it when I get the better of my male colleagues who underestimate me."

She stood up from her rocking chair, and then motioned for Sarah to follow.

"I was just about to make some spaghetti and meatballs. Would you like to join me for dinner?"

Sarah smiled. Looking around, she nodded her head. "Spaghetti and meatballs sounds good right now. What can I do to help?"

Taylour opened the screen door and they walked through to the kitchen. Taylour quickly kicked aside a dirty pair of work boots, picked up some pink socks and tossed them in a corner. "Sorry for the mess. I don't usually have company." Seeing a dark blue t-shirt, she giggled, and caught herself. She scrambled to cover it up with the latest Better Homes & Gardens issue. Taylour scooped up a pile of legal papers that were strewn all over the kitchen counter and set those aside, and then grabbed a pile of tissues and tossed those in the trash can under the sink.

She pulled out the hamburger from the refrigerator, tore the plastic wrapping off, sniffed a frying pan to see if it was clean, and then dumped the meat into it after being reasonably assured that there was no mold or bacteria growing on the surface.

Opening up the refrigerator again, Taylour took out the ingredients and got started. She glanced at Sarah watching in amusement at the whirl of action, and when Taylour turned her back to the stove, Sarah jumped up and grabbed a fork to separate the pasta in the water. She asked Taylour where the olive oil was, and then poured in about one or two tablespoons when the pasta started to boil. The foamy, frothy mixture went down instantly.

They talked as they worked, and Taylour found out that Sarah's parents were still living in Trenton, how she loved to go to a local farm in New Jersey and pick nectarines and raspberries and corn, and how much she missed going into the city. Sarah loved acting and had been in a number of plays when she was in prep school. She also mentioned that she enjoyed going to musicals – her favorite was Miss Saigon, but she didn't care too much for Cats – as well as to the museums, especially the ones focused on art. Her favorite was the Met.

Taylour showed Sarah where the clean dishes were, and Sarah set the table like a pro. She placed the knife on the inside of the spoon on the right, and a napkin folded diagonally and neatly on the left, under the fork, with the folded edge out and the open edge to the right. They took turns putting the food on the table, Taylour asked her if lemonade was OK to drink, and then they sat down.

Just as Taylour was about to pick up her fork and dive in, Sarah asked if she could say grace. Taylour's ears turned red as she nodded her head and closed her eyes. Sarah grabbed Taylour's left hand and started to pray.

"Lord, we thank thee for this meal that thou hast provided, and the hands that have helped prepare it. We thank thee, Father, for all that thou hast given us this day. For old friendships, and new." She squeezed Taylour's hand, and continued.

"Lord, we now ask thee to watch over us, to protect us from evil, and to keep us always on the path of righteousness." Taylour cleared her throat and swallowed. Sarah continued.

"Finally, Lord, we ask thee to--"

The front door slammed open. It rocked the foundation with such force that it nearly broke off the hinges. Men in black streamed in, guns pointing and sweeping the corners. Yells of "Texas Rangers, don't move!" reverberated off the walls. Taylour dived under the table, but Sarah remained seated, unmoving. The lead shooter aimed his weapon squarely at Taylour's head, and then shouted, "Get up! Get up off the floor! Now!"

Taylour hastened to comply, her hands behind her head. "What is going on?"

Sounds of "Clear!" throughout the house, but no one answered Taylour's question, which seemed to hang in the air.

"I demand to know what is going on here!"

"All clear!" yelled the lead shooter, and then a tall man with thick gray hair emerged. He was wearing a nondescript suit and tie, with a slight bump under his right arm. He had a small but distinctive scar on his right temple. He replaced his Glock 17 into his chest holster with his left hand and marched towards Taylour with his badge in his right hand, which he promptly put back in his pocket. Taylour's blood boiled, and just as she was

The Fallen Body

about to let out another protest, he stopped her with his index finger. "Are you Sarah Baines?" he asked.

"What? There's no Sarah Baines--"

"How did you find me?"

They both turned to see Sarah, still seated. Her hands were flat on the table, and she sat unmoving, not from fear, but from acceptance of her fate. She finally pushed herself away and asked again, "How did you find me so quickly?"

The tall man stared at her intently, as if trying to coax some kind of recognition from her, and pulled a photo from his suit pocket. He squinted at the photo, then back at Sarah.

"You changed your hair. It used to be platinum blond, if this picture is accurate." Sarah's hair was black, jet black, and she had it cut to the length of her shoulders. Taylour could see the tiny hints of dryness and dullness, which can come from coloring from a bottle. A feeling of dread came over her. *Who is this person?*

The tall man motioned for Taylour to sit down. "Philip Davidson, Texas Rangers. We have been looking for a fugitive, someone by the name of Sarah Baines, a.k.a. Sarah Cockrell. She is sitting at this table, and I am here to arrest her."

"On what charges, Mr. Davidson?" Taylour said.

"Are you her lawyer?" he smirked.

"As a matter of fact, I am."

Sarah looked at Taylour with pleading in her eyes. Taylour gave her a curt nod, set her jaw, and leaned towards Philip Davidson, staring him straight in the eye.

He squinted right back at Taylour and gave her a hard smile. Without looking in Sarah's direction, he said crisply, "Sarah Cockrell Baines, you are under arrest for the murder of Neal Baines, your husband."

The Fallen Body

Chapter 2

The second movement of Tchaikovsky's Symphony No. 6 "Pathétique" emanated from the cell phone on the nightstand. As the music got louder, a large, hairy hand reached out from under the covers and flipped it open.

After seeing who it was, the figure bolted upright and said, "Hello?"

He listened to the voice on the other end while rubbing and pinching the sleepiness from the inside corners of his dark, brooding eyes.

"I've got a job for you."

The muffled street noises of New York City were all that penetrated the stillness in the lavish 14th floor penthouse. The view from the bedroom faced towards the east, the dull glow of the pre-sunrise sky creating a backdrop to the buildings of Lower Manhattan.

"OK. Who?"

"His name is Neal Baines. I've arranged for your package to be in an envelope under the bench that overlooks the Gapstow Bridge in Central Park. All the details will be there by noon today."

"I will need to pack a bag, yes?"

"Correct, you'll be taking a little trip to Dallas, TX."

The Fallen Body

"And how will I get paid?"

"You'll get half wired to your account this morning, and the other half once the job is done. Your specific instructions will be in your dossier." Click.

He waddled to the bathroom and turned on the hot water to shave. He pulled out his pair of Black Nappa Bruno Maglis and cleaned them with a slightly dampened towelette while whistling to the tune of the TV show "Dallas." He put on his white shirt and tie, and then brushed off his Armani suit jacket with a lint roller. He carefully put on his shoulder holster, adjusted his jacket over the bulge so that it was not so noticeable.

Roman Danshov took the stairs down to the subway and got on the Green Line going towards uptown. He planted himself right next to the door in such a way as to allow himself the luxury of being able to jump off at the last possible moment if he felt that he was being followed. This meant, however, that those passengers getting on and off of the subway had to squeeze past him in order to get around to any available seats. As he held onto one of the stainless steel posts, he ignored the looks that he got from those same commuters. Instead, he scanned the crowd to memorize the faces surrounding him.

At the last moment, Roman jumped off at his stop at Lexington Ave and 59th St and headed against traffic on 59th St. He paused in front of the Banana Republic display to see if anyone was tailing him. When he was satisfied that he was not being followed, he continued passed a GNC and a Clifford Michael tuxedo rental store that was advertising a Going out of Business sale, 60 to 80 percent off.

As he came to Park Ave, he passed the traffic cop at that intersection and crossed over to the other side of the

The Fallen Body

street. Roman stopped in front of the Capital One building, looked through the glass to observe any activity behind him. Seeing nothing, he continued in the same direction as before. The aroma of halal food from a street vendor's cart mixed in with the never ending exhaust made him slightly nauseous, but he continued passed Madison Avenue and the Crate & Barrel store on the corner. As he strode towards 5th Avenue he came to a plaza on the corner on his left, so he cut across to the other side of 59th and strolled around the fountain. He glanced at his watch, which read 11:55 a.m., and decided to sit on the cold, gray marble slab that acted as a bench. The leaves on the trees in the plaza had turned yellow and some had settled on the cement ground.

He paused to observe the traffic around him. He could see the southeast corner of Central Park, which was his ultimate destination, but he was a bit early. As Roman sat in the sun to stay warm, he heard the rustling of the trees and felt the cool breeze on his rugged, unsmiling face. His eyes darted from one person to the next as he waited.

After ten minutes and not seeing anything suspicious, he slowly rose to his feet and crossed the street and entered Central Park. Off to his left he saw an orange school bus disgorge its passengers; a group of elementary kids dressed in their navy blue and white uniforms. He hustled to get past them before they started walking down the trail, most likely going to the Victorian Gardens Amusement Park or the Hallett Nature Sanctuary, both on the other side of the Gapstow Bridge.

He took the path that ran closest to the pond and lowered himself nonchalantly onto the bench that overlooked the eastern portion of The Pond. There were three ducks swimming in the pond, two of them quacking to the third one to keep up, but otherwise the only noise was the rustling of the red oaks in the wind. Turning his head from side to side to see who might be approaching from either direction, he slowly reached his hand underneath where he was sitting. His hand came into contact with an envelope, so he grabbed it from above and removed it from its hiding place. It was a thin, manila package that he hastily rolled up and inserted into the inside pocket of his black overcoat. Roman glanced around one last time, pushed himself off of the bench, and then beat a hasty retreat.

Chapter 3

The buzzing of a chainsaw penetrated the otherwise stillness on the outskirts of Marlinsville. It was a familiar sound in the Texas hill country; farmers clearing out the underbrush that ringed their farmlands in preparation for the few months of winter weather, before it all grew back in the spring. Houses dotted the flat terrain, and those dwellings sheltered hearty folks who worked from dawn to dusk, mostly without complaint. The second and third generations, often times more, tended to their land because that was what their daddy did, and his daddy before him.

Marlinsville was the kind of town that, if you blinked once or twice, you might miss it. There was a large grain mill next to the railroad, the local high school football stadium seated enough to fit the entire population of the county, and everyone had a two-ton pickup as their family car.

Small farm towns like this were scattered from Texas all the way north to Canada, from the edge of the Rocky Mountains in Colorado to the mighty Mississippi River and beyond. The people in these towns represented the heart and soul of America. The economic ups and downs of the country affected these areas the hardest. Yet, one was hard to find anyone willing to give up the peace and serenity that came with living here, at a pace just a little bit slower than the rest of the world.

The chainsaw sputtered to a stop, and Taylour Dixxon set it down to wipe her brow with the back of her hand. She had a habit of wearing a bandana across her forehead to keep the sweat from rolling down into her eyes, but that was already soaked from the day's efforts. In addition to owning nearly ten acres of pristine real estate just outside of town, Taylour was one of a few sole practitioners in the area that practiced small town law. But today, she was putting some "sweat equity" into Dixxon Manor.

The fact that Marlinsville was the county seat of Fallen County meant that the government was the main employer, with farming and ranching right behind. There were long, straight stretches of county roads that both divided the land and connected the residents, many who could trace their roots back to the original settlers of the mid 1800's. Small clapboard churches with small cemetery plots dotted the landscape, with the dusty, gravel parking lot filled on Sunday mornings for Sabbath services and Wednesday evenings for Bible study.

After Taylour bundled up the thinner branches with twine and stacked the thicker trunks against the side of the barn for her fireplace, she collapsed on the front porch steps. Even though she was nearly spent from her exertions, Taylour felt the thrill of a job well done. She took a long, satisfying drink from her thermos and admired her surroundings. There was a small stretch of Bermuda grass that ringed the two-story farmhouse on all sides, between 75-100 feet until the tree line. In the front the ground was hard packed gravel in the rough shape of a horseshoe, which extended from the front porch towards the barn. The barn itself, which acted as a giant tool shed, was in need of a new paint job, but otherwise was in pretty good shape considering the harsh weather it had been through these past 50 years or so. The road from the house passed two Biloxi Crape Myrtles growing on either side, and then meandered around several large oak trees and through tall prairie grass for nearly 150 yards before it met up with the main road going into town.

Taylour loved the view that she had from her porch. She enjoyed lounging in a rocking chair that had been made by hand by her father's father as a gift to her grandmother many years ago. Her grandfather and his new bride were the original occupiers of Dixxon Manor, as it was affectionately called. With his father's help, they built the dwelling themselves, from the foundation up to the rooftop. Over the years Taylour's father renovated the inside structure, room by room, putting in bathrooms with showers, expanded closets and bedrooms, as well as modern appliances in the kitchen and in a new laundry room.

Outside, the dominant hues of golden grain and green leafy crops contrasted sharply with the wide open, brilliant blue skies that were frequently punctuated with white, billowy clouds that more often than not brought much needed rain, but could just as easily bring tornadoes and flash floods. The people of Marlinsville adjusted their lives according to the weather, where being able to predict the patterns was a skill passed on from generation to generation.

Except for when she went to off to college and law school, Taylour had lived her entire life in Marlinsville. Her parents were high school sweethearts who got

The Fallen Body

married young, but they waited to have children while her father, Robert Dixxon went to school, graduating law school from the University of Texas, aka UT Law. He quickly developed a reputation for being both tenacious in defending his clients, as well as caring about what was best for them. He was not afraid to chew out his clients for being abusive or negligent, and then turn right around and offer his services pro bono because he knew that they couldn't afford his fees. It was a difficult balancing act that he was especially good at, and everything he learned he taught to Taylour when she came to work for him when she was only a teenager. Taylour was destined to be an attorney as it was in her blood.

The shadows grew longer with the setting of the sun, so with aching muscles that were in desperate need of a nice, deep massage, Taylour lifted herself off the steps and into the house. She would have to settle for a bubble bath.

As she turned on the water and poured in the bubbles, she stared at herself in the mirror. She had a habit of inspecting for white hairs, which tended to multiply by three for every one that she pulled out. Sigh.

After slipping into the warmth of the bath, she took a wet wash cloth and put it over her face. With her eyes closed, she leaned back on her bath pillow and enjoyed the calm. Her thoughts drifted back to her father, Robert Dixxon.

* * *

Robert knew that Taylour was ready for the difficulties of being a small town lawyer from an incident that occurred right after Taylour joined his practice after passing the bar exam. One day a particularly difficult client of his burst into their office and demanded to speak with "his no-good lawyer" right then and there. Luckily,

~ 16 ~

The Fallen Body

Robert was away at court, or he might have taken the client by the ear and forcefully escorted him out. Well within his rights to do so, but potentially losing the buffoon as a client. Instead, Taylour took the client by the arm, guided him into their small conference room, and listened to what he had to say. She allowed him to go on and on without interruption, occasionally interjecting an "I see…" or an "I understand…" The client, who had expected resistance to his wild accusations of professional misconduct, instead found that everything he said sailed right passed her. Eventually, like a prize fighter who comes out wildly swinging but lands no punches, he fell back into his chair, completely exhausted.

It was at that precise instance that Taylour respectfully delivered a point-by-point rebuttal of his argument, explaining to the client where he was mistaken. Her response had such an effect on the client that he sat up in his chair, hung his head as she talked, and in the end, asked for forgiveness for how he had acted.

Later that night at a public fundraiser for the local library, hosted by the Marlinsville Literary Foundation of which Robert was a board member, he relayed the entire story to Robert and how he had eventually begged Taylour not to drop him as a client. He apologized again for his behavior and handed Robert a $10,000 check made payable to that night's charity.

* * *

Ring! Ring! The sound of the phone on her bedroom nightstand startled Taylour awake. She groaned as she pulled herself out of the tub and wrapped a towel around her. As she lifted the old-fashioned receiver, she looked back at the wet footprints she made on the linoleum and carpet.

"Hello?"

"Is this Taylour Dixxon?"

"Yes, this is she."

"Ms. Dixxon, this is Jim with (inaudible) Services. Are you happy with your current Internet Service Provider?"

"Uh, who is this?"

"This is Jim Edwards from Greentown Telephone Services."

Taylour rolled her eyes. "Jim Edwards from Greentown Telephone Services. Good, I'm writing that down."

"Er, OK. I wanted to--"

"What color eyes do you have? It's Jim, right?"

"Uh, I have blue eyes, but I--"

"Jim, I need to know if you are aware of the National Do Not Call Registry."

"What's that?"

"Oh, good, I'm about to make some money off of you. The National Do Not Call Registry is where individuals, like me, can register their phone numbers so that telemarketers, like you, do not solicit business from us."

"Ms. Dixxon, you're just making this up, aren't you?"

"Could I get your business address?"

"Why do you want my business address?"

"Because your company is about to be served with papers where you, Jim Edwards with blue eyes, and Greentown Telephone Services, will be named as defendants in a lawsuit. See, I'm a lawyer, and all I have to do is--"

Click.

Taylour smiled and put the receiver down.

Chapter 4

After making it into her office early the next morning, Taylour sat down at her desk at her office and pulled out a fresh yellow legal pad. She reveled at the opportunity to try a big case. A murder trial! Finally, something that she could really sink her teeth into. And, the best part? That money was no object.

She had already written down the categories that she needed to organize Sarah's case: People, Documents, Events, Places, and Things. Under People she wrote down the names: Sarah Cockrell Baines (defendant and wife of the deceased), Neil Baines (deceased).

She paused and thought for a moment, and then wrote: Unknown Assailant. She left the rest of that page blank for future names that would come up and then flipped to the next page.

Under Documents she wrote: Warrant for Sarah's arrest, Indictment of Charges, and Motions, and then turned to the next page.

She scribbled: Events, and then listed Prior to Murder, Date of Murder, and Arrest of Sarah.

The Fallen Body

She continued with Places and Things on the subsequent pages, composing a list of relevant items that she knew.

After she was done, she sighed and rubbed her forehead as she felt a headache coming on. There is so little that I know at this point.

Finally, she wrote down an action plan and a timeframe for each item. Taylour wanted to hire a private investigator, and that took money. She turned around to her computer, typed and clicked until she came to her bank balance, and then sighed again. The headache intensified.

Taylour heard the tingling of the bell hanging from the front door, and then a distant thump as Betty, her secretary/paralegal, dropped her purse down next to the front desk. She looked up as Betty walked down the hall towards Taylour's office and turned into the kitchen.

Taylour yelled good morning and got a less than enthusiastic response back, so she called for Betty to come into her office.

"Is anything wrong?"

"Uh, no. Everything's fine. It's just bills and personal stuff."

"Is there anything that I can do to help you?"

Betty lowered her gaze and turned away. "Nah, there's nothing going on."

Taylour persisted. "Come on, I can tell when something is bothering you."

"Really, I'm fine!"

Taylour lifted her hands up as if to surrender. "OK, then. I won't bother you."

Betty cleared her throat and changed the subject. "You have your bond hearing for Sarah today, right?"

The Fallen Body

"Correct." Taylour looked at her watch and stood up. "I should be back in time for my afternoon appointments." She picked up her briefcase and swept past Betty. "Oh, I almost forgot. I need to hire a private investigator to do some digging around in New Jersey. Can you find me one that I can talk to this afternoon? I want to give them some particulars, but I won't have them until after talking with Sarah today."

"Sure thing. I've got a cousin in the Newark Police Department who I'm sure can recommend someone."

"Your cousin Theo, right? The one who got shot in the leg last year?"

"That's the one. His poor mother, bless her heart, had to take care of him, being that he wasn't married and had no one else. He has a desk job now, but I'm sure that he can recommend a private eye."

Taylour said thanks and pushed on the door to leave the office when Betty called out to her.

"Hey, I almost forgot. Mr. Burton called for you last week." A blast of cold air entered in, which caused Betty to shiver. She pulled her black cardigan off of the back of her chair and wrapped it around her shoulders.

Taylour stopped in her tracks. "Why didn't you —"

"Sorry, I meant to tell you, I just, uh, forgot. He sounded like he was just checking in on you. No big deal."

Taylour dropped what she was carrying and sat down. She quickly dialed a number, got a recorded voice, and left a short message for Mr. Burton to call her back on her cell phone. She wondered why he hadn't called her directly, since he certainly had her cell number. She shrugged her shoulders, and then grabbed her things and quickly left.

Chapter 5

Taylour glanced around the magistrate's office in the Frank Crowley Court Building on Industrial Blvd in downtown Dallas while she waited for Sarah. This was her first time in this place as an attorney, and she felt uncertain as she doodled on her pad of paper. There was tenseness in her stomach and a constant craving for water to quench her thirst. Her mind raced through the possibilities of Sarah being released on bail.

The only good thing working in Sarah's favor was that she was a first-time felony offender. Otherwise, she had a lot more going against her. Sarah was from out of town, she was a flight risk and had the financial means to go anywhere she wanted, and the nature of the crime was sufficiently severe that, faced with anywhere from 5 to 99 years in prison – the penalty for first degree murder in Texas – Sarah will be considered to be someone inclined to skip out on her bail.

Taylour spent the few moments deciding on a course of action, but then she started second guessing herself. Should I lead with the need to take care of her elderly parents? But they are back in New Jersey, so that won't be a possibility as the magistrate is sure to restrict her movements.

She turned as she heard the jangling of the iron bands that Sarah had on both her wrists and ankles. Sarah stood tensely in front of her, her eyes bulging out and unblinking.

"H-Hi, Taylour," she said as her chin and lips trembled.

Taylour gave Sarah an awkward hug and cringed inside. *Poor thing, she looks so lost and out of place here.*

"Sarah, everything is going to be OK. You look great. Keep your chin up."

Sarah smiled despite herself. "I look horrible! My hair is ratty," she said while touching her head with both hands, the handcuffs getting in the way, "and I-I haven't had a decent shower since before our dinner on Monday. That seems like so long ago. I-I just want to get out of here."

"I understand. This bond hearing is merely a formality. There's a very good chance that you will be released."

"W-What happens after that?"

"If you are allowed to leave on bail, then we prepare for the indictment from the grand jury. The prosecution must submit sufficient evidence of a crime to them for the grand jury to issue a written statement accusing you, as the defendant, of murdering your husband."

Sarah gasped and expelled her breath as if in pain. She closed her eyes and her knees started to buckle. She reached out to Taylour, who grabbed her under her arm and guided her to a seat.

"W-We can't let that happen, Taylour!" She clutched Taylour's arm and her knuckles turned white from her grasp.

The Fallen Body

Taylour grabbed Sarah's hands and held them in her own in an effort to calm Sarah down.

"Everything is going to work itself out."

"I didn't murder my husband, Taylour. You have to believe me!"

Taylour wanted to tell Sarah that it didn't matter if she believed Sarah to be innocent or not, but that seemed inadequate, so Taylour squeezed Sarah's hands tightly and said, "Sarah, I have only known you a short time, but I do believe you to be a good, decent person." She positioned her gaze on Sarah until Sarah locked her eyes on Taylour. "I don't think you are capable of such a horrible action, and I will do everything, *everything,* in my power to see this through to the end."

Sarah's eyes went moist and tears rolled down her cheeks. She sniffed and gave a nervous laugh. She leaned into Taylour and rested her head on Taylour's shoulder. There she remained until the magistrate marched into the room, her robes swishing as she made her way to her padded chair on the dais. All present in the room arose, and then sat down when Chief Magistrate Sherrie McMann motioned them to take their seats.

As the magistrate reviewed the paperwork, Taylour's eyes drifted to her legal opponent: late twenties, six foot two, thick, dark-blonde hair partially greased at the front and the sides. He reminded her of a young Ryan Reynolds, only more attractive.

She dropped her gaze, cleared her throat a bit too loudly, and whipped her head back towards the front. The magistrate, misinterpreting the noise, looked over her reading glasses and asked sternly, "Are we in a hurry, counselor?"

"Uh, n-no, your Honor, I just, ah… Never mind. Take your time."

The Fallen Body

"Why thank you, counselor. I appreciate your magna-*nim*-ity. Ms. Dixxon, is it?" Her steely gaze bore holes into Taylour.

Not a good idea to start the case on the judge's bad side. Great job, Taylour!

Taylour almost cleared her throat again, but this time she managed to stay silent. She nodded her head in agreement.

Hon. McMann opened her mouth as if to reprimand her again for not verbalizing her agreement, but instead, turned to the prosecution table and smiled a warm smile.

"Mr. Stedman, it is good to see you again so soon. I hope your mother is doing better. Tsk, tsk."

Jake Stedman grinned back at the magistrate and included Taylour in his response. "Thankfully, she is feeling much better. When I told her that I was going to see you this morning, she insisted that I pass along this thank you card. May I approach the bench?"

"Yes, of course!"

Mr. Stedman drew a small envelope from his coat pocket and approached the rostrum. He handed it to the magistrate, exchanged a few hushed words with her, and then they both laughed. Mr. Stedman took his place again behind the desk.

Taylour silently groaned and started fidgeting in her seat. While this was only a bond hearing and Taylour had attended many of them, she did not like how this was proceeding.

Finally, after what seemed an eternity, but had only been a few minutes, Hon. McMann asked the accused to stand, which she did with Taylour by her side.

After clearing her throat, the magistrate stared down at Sarah, gave her a perfunctory smile, and then recited from memory a list of things for Sarah.

The Fallen Body

The magistrate explained that Sarah was accused of the murder of her husband, that she had a right to retain counsel, and that she had the right to have an attorney present during any interview with a peace officer or the attorney representing the prosecution.

"You may also terminate any interview at any time. Also, you have a right to an examining trial, and a jury made up of your peers, so don't take that opportunity lightly."

Hon. McMann leaned in as if she were about to tell a little secret. "Finally, you have the right to remain silent. Any statements that you make can be used against you. Do you understand your rights as I have explained them to you?"

Sarah nodded and said yes.

"Thank you. Now, we will proceed with the arguments related to bail."

Hon. McMann motioned for the prosecutor to start.

Mr. Stedman rose from his desk. "Your Honor, due to the nature of the crime, the lack of any family ties in the community, the fact that the defendant made herself unavailable for questioning after the murder of her husband by her sudden disappearance, and that she has substantial assets in her name, we ask that the accused be denied bail and remain behind bars."

The judge looked over the two attorneys and asked Mr. Stedman a question. "Do you consider Ms. Sarah Cockrell Baines to be a flight risk?"

"Yes, your Honor, we do, given the fact that she escaped to Marlinsville, TX suddenly and without warning."

Taylour jumped from her seat. "Your Honor, the fact that the accused *escaped* to Marlinsville can be explained. She recently inherited property in Marlinsville and was simply taking care of things in town. While she didn't walk into the District Attorney's office and give herself up for questioning, there is no evidence that she tried to hide or flee from the authorities." Taylour sat back down.

Hon. McMann rested her chin on her hands in thought, and then asked Taylour, "Counselor, what do you deem to be an appropriate course of action at this time?"

Taylour was surprised to be asked this so soon. Usually the opportunity to present her side came after a more vigorous argument from the prosecution. She shuffled some papers on her desk and slowly rose up from her spot. "Your Honor, while my client does have some funds at her disposal, a number of her bank accounts and other assets are held jointly with her husband. The settlement of Mr. Baines estate is nowhere near completion, especially since he died under auspicious circumstances, and the release of those accounts may take months or even years while the search for the real killer is completed."

"Careful, counselor. You needn't testify on your client's behalf just yet." Hon. McMann lifted her chin off of her hands and grabbed the gavel. "The court sets bail at $250,000." *Thump,* came the sound from her dais, and then she let go of the handle.

They were dismissed. Taylour took Sarah aside and explained the process for posting bail, either through a surety bond or by paying cash that would be held until the end.

"Taylour, whatever it takes, I will do it. I don't want to spend any more time in jail than I have to."

"I understand. You need to call your parents."

The Fallen Body

"I know that I need to talk with my parents, but... I'm afraid about what this news will do to them. My mom is not in good health, and my dad can barely take care of both of them." Sarah sniffed back her tears. "I-I just need to figure out a way to get past this before I tell them."

"Sarah, it is unreasonable to assume that this can be resolved quickly. You are accused of murdering your husband!"

"But I didn't do it!"

This time, Taylour didn't hold back. "Whether you did it or not, that is immaterial at this point. The police had probable cause in asking for a warrant to arrest you. That is a long way from showing that you are innocent." She reached her hand out and put it on Sarah's arm. "That does not happen quickly, and if you want to get out of jail while we prepare for trial, you are going to have to involve your parents."

Taylour shuffled some papers together and put them in her briefcase. "We also need to talk about everything that happened that night. I am going to let them take you back, and then I'll come and visit you, OK?"

Sarah took a deep breath in and nodded, the fear on her face coming back as she must have realized the enormity of the situation. As the guards led her away, she turned her head around. Taylour gave her a big smile and nodded her head while mouthing the words, "You're gonna be OK." Sarah's plaintive smile cut straight through Taylour's heart.

"It's gonna be OK." Taylour said to herself, the ache in her chest not easily forgotten.

Chapter 6

W. Hunter "Bulldog" Burton, Jr. was a former JAG-attorney-turned-litigator and Robert Dixxon's closest friend and ally. The two of them had met as opposing counsels in a messy custody dispute between a high-ranking naval officer, his faithful wife of thirty years, and his mistress, who happened to be one of his aides at the time that the affair was discovered. Robert had represented the wife and Bulldog had stood in for the naval officer. After months of legal maneuvering where neither party gained the upper hand, the case was finally settled in arbitration. While the officer's reputation was sullied by the affair and his mistress left him soon after the divorce, things could have been much worse for him as he was spared from spending time in prison for putting the nation's secrets at risk. The wife was awarded the majority of their joint possessions and exacted her own revenge when she married a minor football legend almost twenty years her junior who doted on her hand and foot.

Robert and Bulldog had been close ever since.

Bulldog and his lovely wife Charlotte were frequent guests of the Dixxon home whenever the Burtons were in town, and Robert played a pivotal role in convincing

The Fallen Body

Bulldog to move his family to Central Texas after Bulldog's service as a Judge Advocate General. He and his wife gladly accepted the unofficial role of godparents to Taylour and Vincent, and Robert and Doris Dixxon could think of no other couple, including their own family, who they trusted more to take care of their children if something were to happen to them.

After the Burtons moved to Texas, the two friends never again faced off against each other in cases that were brought to their attention. They would often refer clients to each other if it was out of their respective expertise. While Robert mainly focused on general family law, Bulldog made a name for himself in injuries, tort and workman's comp cases. More than once they had to recuse themselves for personal reasons if the other was the named counsel of the opposing party. Both of them were willing to lose out on hourly billings because neither was willing to jeopardize their ongoing friendship. That all changed when Robert was killed in a car accident.

Robert was driving home late one winter night during a rare snow storm. He was cautiously navigating the icy roads when he was suddenly overtaken from behind. The driver of the other vehicle had just turned 21 and had been celebrating his new found "freedom" by drinking shots of whiskey with his friends at the bar on the edge of town. Robert's Toyota Corolla was no match for the Super Duty Ford F-150 King Ranch when it was tapped from behind. While the force of the collision was almost inconsequential, because of the black ice that had formed at that precise spot, the Corolla spun around, flipped over a few times, and then landed upside down in the ditch on the side of the road. The truck barely slowed down from the collision, and the driver sped away without offering any assistance.

The Fallen Body

Forensic evidence at the scene had been mostly compromised by the storm by the time the crash had been discovered, and the lead crime scene investigator who had worked the accident believed it to be caused by the weather.

The autopsy report indicated that Robert had suffered from "blunt force trauma" after having come in "violent contact with the inside ceiling" of his car. The official cause of death was massive blood loss from his head wounds, which meant that Robert did not die quickly.

The driver of the other vehicle never came forward, most likely because his recollection of the night was glazed over from the drunken stupor he had been in. Bulldog had made it his mission in life to find out what really happened that night as he was not convinced it had been an accident caused by the weather. He had followed up on several leads, all of which had dried up faster than a cornfield under the hot, Texas sun, but he didn't have the nickname of Bulldog for nothing.

Years had passed since the accident, and Taylour, busy with maintaining her practice after the death of her father, still clung to the hope that the truth about her father's death would come to light. While she and Bulldog often talked about her cases and his family, their conversation inevitably turned towards the subject of her father's untimely demise.

He had not called while Taylour had been in court. She was anxious to know if Bulldog had found a new clue about her father.

Chapter 7

After running some errands in downtown Dallas, Taylour entered the county jail where Sarah was being held. An antiseptic smell hung in the air as Taylour was led to a private conference room. She pulled out a fresh legal notepad and labeled it with Sarah Cockrell Baines and today's date. When the door opened, Taylour stood up and went to Sarah. She asked the female guard to remove the handcuffs, which she did, and then Taylour thanked the guard, who indicated that she would be right outside.

Sarah sat erect on her chair as she faced Taylour. Again with the stiff posture. It suggested to Taylour that Sarah was in a societal class much higher than her own. Taylour did not have a lot of experience with urbanites like Sarah, but the scales of justice were blind to class and stature, at least in Taylour's mind. In order for her to provide a more than adequate defense was to know everything that there was to know about the case, and that always started with knowing the client. If the client was forthright and honest about everything, then she could formulate the best strategy going forward. Too often, however, client's held things back, which was never a good thing.

"Sarah, what I want you to do is to tell me about the night that Neal died, OK?"

The night that Neal died, Sarah asked herself, "Is my husband really having an affair?" Sarah clenched and unclenched her hands on the steering wheel. As she followed her husband's taxi to downtown Dallas, she put the pieces together. The furtive glances when taking a phone call, the unexplained absences away from their home in the posh neighborhood of Alpine, NJ, the hint of someone else's perfume on his shirts. All seemingly innocent by themselves, but when put together, they spelled only one thing. Another woman.

While he had been working long hours at the office of one of the most prestigious law firms in New York City, Kostas, Marchese & Rowe, Sarah had been taking care of her ailing parents in Trenton, NJ. She winced as she remembered the early signs of Alzheimer's in her mother, Janice Cockrell, a proud, stubborn, Irish woman! Sarah felt the hot tears on her cheeks and an aching in her chest as she realized that her time with her mother was slipping away. She turned away briefly, took a deep breath, and set her jaw. That doesn't give him the right to cheat on me! Her eyes turned cold, hard, and flinty.

She continued to follow her husband's taxi, sure that she wasn't being noticed as she followed in her rental car, a 2012 gray Chevrolet Impala. His taxi pulled up to The Tower Residences in downtown Dallas, TX. His 5'10" frame slid smoothly from the back seat, and he thanked the driver for helping him unload his luggage by extending him a sizable tip. Sarah drove past the entrance and parked her car in the first row closest to the building. She waited several moments, drawing in slow, steady breaths, and looked over at her purse. She opened it up and reached inside for the .22.

She held it in her hand, turning it slowly so that she could get the feel of it. Her hand shook as she gripped the handle, her finger hovering over the trigger guard. She stuffed the gun back into her purse and got out of the car. She thrust her chin forward and slammed the car door.

As she approached the entrance, she felt the wind kick up, messing up her platinum blonde hair. She snuck in past the doorman and skittered over to the elevator, pushed the Up button, and entered without looking back.

Her nostrils flared and she curled her lips. The veins in her neck pulsed as she paced back and forth inside the elevator car. A single bell announced her arrival as the doors slid open.

She thrust her hand in her purse and pulled out the .22. She held it behind her back as she pounded hard on the door.

She stomped her feet impatiently and flexed her fingers. The peephole darkened, and then the chain on the other side was unlocked. The door flew open.

"Honey, what are you doing here? I wasn't expecting--"

Sarah barreled past him and into the dining room. The table was set for two, a lit candle gave off a wistful light, and a bottle of wine was placed gently in a bed of ice. She smelled garlic bread in the oven, and heard Harry Connick, Jr. singing "We are In Love" on the stereo. That was all the evidence that she needed.

She turned to him and pointed the gun at his chest. "How can you do this to me?"

"Hey, now, sweetie, uh... let's put the gun down and we can talk about this." Neal nearly tripped over the corner of the hallway rug as he slowly backed away from Sarah.

"You want to talk about this? This?" She waved the gun at him unsteadily, and then placed her left hand over her right.

"Sarah, let's not make any hasty conclusions. I am having a guest over, yes, but it is not what you think."

"And what do I think, Neal? That you are meeting one of your clients for a nice, romantic dinner in your penthouse? That is exactly what this is!" She took a step toward him and he backed away, his two hands raised with his palms out.

The Fallen Body

"Whoa, wait a minute, what makes you think that? What makes you think that I wasn't secretly expecting you to show up?"

Sarah's nostrils flared and her muscles strained against her skin. "You knew that I was going to spend the weekend at my parent's house. You knew that you were going to be alone here, so you invited one of your clients to keep you company. What's her name, Neal?"

"Hold on, that's not fair. You know that I would never cheat on you! I love you."

"You love me? Then what is all this?" Sarah swept her arm around the room. "This apartment is new to me. I didn't know that you had it."

"It's not even mine, Sarah. Look, the firm has apartments like this in several cities, for attorneys that are from out of town."

"Then who are you having dinner with?"

"Look, let's just put the gun down and I will explain everything, OK?" Neal moved slowly towards her.

She couldn't do it. "I-I'd better go." She turned and went unsteadily to the door.

She turned back to look at Neal. "Do you still love me, Neal?"

With shaky laughter, he responded, "Of course, Sarah. Of course I do." He reached out his hand to her and placed it on her shoulder. She felt the heat rising from his touch, and then fell into his outstretched arms, sobbing.

"Neal, I'm so sorry. I... just thought..." She sniffled back the tears, brushed away at the lipstick spot she had just made on his shoulder. "Sorry, I just made a mess of your shirt." She backed away, and said, "Will you call me when you are done? I want to talk... about us. I'm just going to clear my head. You do what you have to tonight, and we'll talk more, OK?"

"OK. Give me about an hour to talk business with my client, and then I will call you. I promise." Neal gazed at his wife, and *said, "I love you. Everything is going to be alright." He kissed her softly on her forehead.*

"I love you too," she said, with resolve. She turned away and Neal closed the door.

As she exited the building, Sarah reached into her purse, touched the cold steel of the gun with her fingers, and then pulled her hand out as if she had just been burned. She walked past a man in a dark sedan, who studied her from the instant that she exited. She glanced around, saw a garbage can, and dumped the gun. She wasn't going to use it after all.

Taylour furiously scribbled her notes as Sarah went along. After Sarah described leaving the parking lot the night of his death, Taylour changed the topic.

"What do you know about Neal's work?"

"Not much, he didn't like to bring it up when we were together."

"And you never asked?"

Sarah looked like she was about to cry again, so Taylour covered Sarah's hand with her own and said, "I'm sorry, I didn't mean to upset you."

"It's OK, I don't know what has come over me. I almost never cry about things, but now I'm crying all the time."

"What you are facing, this whole situation, it can be very overwhelming to people, especially to those who are innocent."

Sarah wiped her eyes. "It's just hard, you know, to have to not only deal with his death, but to be accused of something that I didn't do, and the regrets that I have. Just everything, together, makes it hard for me to... to function like normal."

Taylour lowered her head to get Sarah to look into her eyes. "I promise you, we will get through this. I know that it seems like the world is caving in around you, but you can overcome this. The most important thing to remember is that you are not alone. I'm here whenever you need me, and I will do everything in my power to get you out."

Taylour jotted down a note. "While we work on getting you out on bail, we are going to need to hire a private investigator. That is going to require funds." Taylour put her pen down and clasped her hands together.

"Sarah, are you familiar with the concept of a retainer?"

"Uh, I think so. I provide you with a certain amount of money so that you work for me, correct?"

"That is the general concept. It is specifically used to pay for my future services to see a case through to its conclusion. It can either be a lump sum amount or recurring monthly payments, and any amount that is not used can be returned." Taylour pulled her standard retainer agreement out, which she had filled in previously, and slid that across the table to Sarah.

"I will pay whatever it takes. I trust you." Sarah signed her name at the bottom without even glancing at the contract.

Chapter 8

The next morning, Sarah was allowed to call her parents. She had rehearsed in her mind what she wanted to say, but that was not going to make it any easier. As she slowly dialed the number to her parents, she took a deep breath, filled up her lungs, and then exhaled slowly to calm herself. She did not want to put her parents through this ordeal, but it was necessary that they be in the loop. Her knuckles turned white as she gripped the phone, the dull beeping from the other end piercing through her as she waited and waited.

Finally, after nine or ten rings, it stopped ringing. "H-Hello?" came the weak reply. It was her father.

"Hey, dad, it's me, Sarah." She sniffed softly.

"Sarah! It's so good to hear from you! Your mother and I were worried when you hadn't called these last few weeks. Is everything OK?"

Sarah paused for a moment. "Ah, well, everything is not OK, dad." Sarah tried to speak, but the only noise that came out was a squeak. She took another deep breath and managed to say, "Neal's dead, and they think I did it."

"What? Neal's dead?" Sarah could hear her mother in the background yelling at her father to tell her what was going on, so he whispered into the phone, "Sarah, what do you mean they think you did it?"

Sarah heard the panic in her father's voice. "Dad, I can't talk about that right now. I need you to contact my attorney and she will explain everything, OK?"

She heard her father ask her mother for a pen and paper, and then, "What's the number?" His voice sounded more authoritative this time, his old police instincts finally kicking in.

As she gave him the number, she added, "Her name is Taylour Dixxon, and she lives in Marlinsville, Texas."

A brief pause, and then, "Have you been staying at your old Aunt Edna's place?"

"Yes, I had some work to do to get the place all fixed up and ready to sell, s-so I came down after Neal..."

"Sarah, it's OK, everything is going to be fine. I'll contact your attorney and we'll make all the necessary arrangements."

Sarah gave her father all of the particulars of how to contact Taylour, and then asked about her mother, who was doing fine.

"Th-Thanks, dad. I am so sorry about all of this!" she managed to say before hanging up. With her back up against the cold concrete wall, she slid down onto the floor. She put her face in her hands and sobbed.

Chapter 9

Taylour hung up with Mr. Cockrell and rubbed her eyes. Conversations with family members of her clients were almost always difficult, and this one was no exception. The line between providing relevant information while trying to maintain the attorney/client privilege was a balancing act that required both courage on her part and confidence that she didn't always have. Mr. Cockrell had peppered her with questions about everything, the crime scene, the murder weapon, had there been any witnesses, what is the disposition of the district attorney, is there anyone else with a motive. All reasonable questions, but all ones that she did not have the answers to nor could she speculate.

She explained that Sarah had been asked to put up bail for $250,000, which Mr. Cockrell said was no problem, Sarah had the funds and he would make the arrangements to get the money together. Towards the end, the conversation had turned to her experience in defending a client accused of murder, and Taylour admitted to him that she had never defended someone in that situation. He seemed reluctant when he hung up despite her assurances that she would do everything in her power to help their daughter.

Taylour's thoughts were interrupted when she heard the jangle of bell that hung over the front door of their law practice. When she glanced at her watch, she inwardly groaned at the time. Her first appointment was with the father of a young man, Cliff Johnson, who was accused of driving while intoxicated. This was his third arrest, and because he was a repeat offender, the chances of him getting bail were slim.

However, the booming voice that came from the front was not Mr. Johnson, but from her neighbor, George Frockmeier. Curious, she poked her head out of her private office to see if she was right and almost got run over as Mr. Frockmeier came barreling down the hall.

"Ms. Dixxon, I need your help. My wife and I--"

"Mr. Frockmeier, I'm sorry to interrupt you, but I have an appointment at--"

"I know, I saw him getting out of his truck as I came in. I just need a minute of your time. As I was saying, my wife and I were talkin' yesterday about my brother, who's not doin' too well, on account of him having cancer, and we, we were wondering about our wills and are they up-to-date with all that's been goin' on, so Barbara asked me if I knew where they were, and I told her that I thought she had them as she does all the filing, but she didn't know where they were, so I said to her, Barbara, I have to go to town tomorrow, I'll just ask Ms. Dixxon for a copy. So, can I have a copy?"

"Betty here can help you with that, Mr. Frockmeier, OK?" Taylour walked him back towards the front and turned him over to Betty. She then turned to Mr. Johnson, who had a mean scowl on his face, and greeted him with a firm handshake. She learned at an early age

The Fallen Body

that if you squeeze a man's hand, he'll take you more seriously. He did not squeeze back.

"Mr. Johnson, if you will please follow me to my office, we can get started."

Once they were in her office, she motioned for him to sit down as she closed the door.

"Who does he think he is, pushin' his way past me so that he can get here first. I have an appointment."

"Yes, Mr. Johnson, I am sorry about that." He gave her another scowl, but this time he said nothing. "Let's talk about getting your son out on bail."

"Don't know why we have to keep doin' this, the boy don't mean no harm."

"Mr. Johnson, Cliff was pulled over by the sheriff after taking out a part of Mr. Henderson's white picket fence and mailbox. When the sheriff--"

"That no-good sheriff, he has it out for my boy!" Mr. Johnson yelled. "That fence needs replacin' anyhow."

Taylour thought for a moment, and then asked, "Are you saying that Cliff is willing to pay to fix the fence and mailbox? If that's the case, I'll take that to the judge to see if he can be released on his own recognizance."

"Don't need to pay someone to fix it, he can do that hisself. We ain't got the money, but Cliff, he's a hard worker. He ain't the smartest tool in the shed, but he's just a teenager."

"So, how do you propose getting the funds so that he can purchase the materials?"

Mr. Johnson rubbed his chin with his rough, weathered hand. His fingernails were overdue for a trimming and the grease and dirt seemed permanently blended into the creases of his fingers. "I got a few spare boards that he can use, along with some paint. Would that work?"

The Fallen Body

"What about the mailbox?"

"It's just dented s'all. I can take it to my shop and fix 'er up all nice an' new."

"Great! I'll get the paperwork prepared. If Mr. Henderson agrees to your terms, I'll get everything signed by the judge and Cliff can be released this evening."

"Er, can y' make it tomorrow instead?"

Taylour furrowed her brow and asked, "Why?"

Mr. Johnson shifted in his seat and his face flushed a bright red. "Well, Ms. Dixxon, it's, ah, well, the missus and I, it's our anniversary today."

"Congratulations! How many years have you been married?"

"Oh, it's been 'bout twenty five years. See, we were fixin' to go out to Rudy's All-You-Can Eat for dinner tonight, and, well..."

"And?" Taylour suppressed a smile as Mr. Johnson squirmed in his chair. She managed to keep a straight face as he continued.

"Well, we would like to, to have some time to, to be alone, Ms. Dixxon. We never seem to get any time to--"

"Say no more, Mr. Johnson, I get the picture." She turned around to her computer and pretended to type something so that she could regain her composure. With her back still turned, she managed to blurt out, "I'll see that the judge gets this tomorrow afternoon."

"Thank y' kindly, Ms. Dixxon." He stood up to leave and Taylour escorted him to the front door. This time when he shook her hand, he squeezed it harder than before, pumping it up and down. "Thank y' Ms. Dixxon, thank y' so much!"

"Have a wonderful anniversary, Mr. Johnson." She stood there at Betty's desk and waited until he had pulled out of the parking lot, and then Taylour burst out laughing, nearly falling over onto the floor. After Betty's puzzled look, Taylour recounted what had just transpired, after which Betty guffawed as well.

"He deserves to squirm, that ol' coot," Betty said.

Chapter 10

Detective Jack Foreman had a problem, and he didn't know what to do about it. The problem had to do with the Neal Baines' murder investigation, to which he and his junior partner, Jillian Severly, had been assigned. As he sat at his desk holding a cup of coffee that, at best, was lukewarm, he ran the case through his head. It was an uncomfortable thing for him, to feel one way and to have acted against that same feeling.

While he knew that there was evidence that showed Ms. Baines was in the apartment right before the murder, this evidence in his mind was circumstantial. The gun that they had recovered from the scene had her fingerprints on it, and yes, she had fled the scene, but without additional proof, such as witness corroboration or her side of the story, they barely had a reasonable suspicion to arrest her. Any first year law student could find logical explanations for such findings. It was against Jack's better judgment that the DA had gone ahead with arresting Sarah, but he had.

But what about the body of her husband being tossed over the balcony? Ms. Baines was not a strong enough woman capable of doing that, so did she have

The Fallen Body

help? And what about the witness testimony of the doorman, who said that he doesn't remember seeing her as she came in or as she left? Could she have killed him and someone else dropped the body from the 20th floor minutes later? The coroner's report couldn't find the exact cause of death. Was it the two bullets in the chest? Or was it the fall from twenty stories up? The video tape showed her entering the elevator and going to Mr. Baines' apartment. It also showed her leaving Mr. Baines' apartment and exiting the building 10 minutes later. The initial review of the video did not show anyone else going to Mr. Baines' apartment, at least by the elevator.

There was something about the video that he couldn't quite put his finger on. He chugged the rest of his coffee, and then proceeded to the crime lab.

"Hey, Jillian, y' wanna come down to the lab with me? Something just ain't sitting right with me."

Jillian looked up from the paperwork that she was doing and nodded her head. "Sure, I'll come." She fell in line behind him and quickened her pace to keep up.

They went down the elevator and turned to the right once they reached the 3rd floor. Jack knocked on the sound room door and a technician on the other side opened it up and ushered them in.

"We'd like to see the elevator footage again on the Baines' case." Jack said.

The technician, Mitchell Deebler, said, "Didn't we go over that already?"

"Yeah, but something keeps buggin' me. Start with the part where she enters the elevator."

Mitchell rewound the video player, and in an instant they were looking at a sharp, black and white video feed of the lobby, with the time stamp of 18:51:00, or exactly 6:51 p.m.

The Fallen Body

They observed residents getting on and off of the elevator, and then Ms. Baines came into view at 18:52:05. Mitchell slowed the frames to see if anything jumped out at them, but nothing special showed up.

"OK, now let's look at the footage of the 20th floor when she gets off."

Mitchell pushed some buttons, and the camera angle switched to the 20th floor. The camera on that floor pointed to the small alcove of the apartment on the opposite side from Mr. Baines' apartment. They watched Ms. Baines exit the elevator and move out of view as she went to number 2001.

Jack jumped out of his chair and pointed to the top corner of the picture. "What is that?"

Mitchell zoomed in to where Jack was pointing, which appeared to be the bottom corner of a large mirror. The mirror caught the reflection of Ms. Baines' shoe as she stood in the opposite doorway, out of view, and then it disappeared, most likely because she entered Mr. Baines' apartment. Mitchell then pushed the fast forward button so that they could accelerate the timeframe until Ms. Baines' came out. They did not observe anyone on that floor during the time that Ms. Baines was in the apartment. When the three of them looked at the time stamp, it indicated 18:59:23, which was about seven minutes later. Still enough time to shoot someone, but not enough time to drag the body over to the balcony and toss it over the side. Mitchell switched back to the lobby video, and then they watched her leave the building. She left at 19:01:07, which was almost sixteen minutes before Mr. Baines' body fell to the ground at about 19:17:00.

Exasperated, Jack wrung his hands together, and then he had an idea. "Keep playing the video of the 20th floor, after Ms. Baines leaves." Mitchell started that video at 19:01:00.

As the video played, Jack kept his eyes focused on the corner of the mirror. One minute went by, then two, and then three.

Nothing.

After nine minutes had passed, Jack slumped into his chair, wondering if his hunch might be wrong. It was at 19:10:45 that he saw what he was looking for.

In the mirror, there was a clear image of a large, black shoe, and then it disappeared, just like Ms. Baines' had minutes before.

"That's a Bruno Magli shoe..." said Jillian as they all looked at each other.

Mitchell said, "Someone else went into Mr. Baines' apartment…"

"Do you realize that this is a major screw-up of epic proportions?" Jack said.

One of them was going to have to tell the District Attorney about this latest discovery, and none of them were looking forward to that conversation.

"Let's take this to the lieutenant," Jack said softly. "Maybe he can break the news to the DA."

* * *

Things moved swiftly after that. After dressing down the two detectives and Mitchell for their initial shoddy work, the lieutenant calmed down, thanked them for what they discovered, and then dismissed them from his office. He took the information to the captain, who then called the DA at his home. When the DA heard the news, he politely thanked the captain for passing on the news, hung up, and then resisted the urge to throw his phone through the wall. As he pondered his next move, he drew doodles on the notepad and weighed his options.

The Fallen Body

He developed a plan, and then he shot off an email to his secretary to block some time the next morning with Ms. Dixxon. If he could get Ms. Baines to agree to tell everything that she knew, then he would drop the charges against her.

The DA rubbed his eyes in an effort to push out the strain. Back to square one.

Chapter 11

As Taylour drove to her office that morning, she mentally went down her list of things to do. The restroom and kitchen both needed a good mopping, and the carpet was due for vacuuming. Maybe she could get Betty to come in early on Friday to help. She shook her head and gave a rueful smile. Betty hated to clean almost as much as she did, including the day-to-day maintenance of picking up the trash and taking it out to the side dumpster. Getting her to do more than that would definitely require a dozen freshly glazed donuts from the Krispy Kreme that recently opened in their strip mall. It was a great spot for it, actually. People visited their loved ones in the cemetery right next to her law office, and then, realizing that life was short, they continued their mourning by getting a jolt of good, old fashioned carbohydrates.

Taylour was already a frequent customer.

She thought about all of the different cases she was juggling and what items were critical and which were less critical. The thing is, when it came to her clients' freedom and their hard earned money, all problems were critical. She gave a huge sigh and wished for more time in the day.

The Fallen Body

As she got out of her car, the aroma of fried dough assaulted her, almost pushing her back into her car to make the short trip through the drive-thru. They make it so easy! Before you could even feel guilty about buying them, you had them, sitting next to you in the passenger seat. She glanced wistfully at the line of cars and determined that there were very few sad people that ever drove away from that place.

The clanging of the bell over the door snapped her out of her reverie when she pulled it open. She hurried to close it behind her, thus blocking the temptation from her mind.

It was still early for Betty to be there, so Taylour pushed the button to listen to the recordings left on the answering machine. The light indicated three new messages. Taylour listened to each of them, jotted down the names and numbers, and then strode to her private office down the hall.

Just as she was about to enter her office, the phone rang again, so she hurried to her desk and pushed the line to answer.

"Hello?"

"Please hold the line for District Attorney Paul Justin." The sounds of a string quartet came on for a brief moment, which allowed Taylour to sit down and fire up her computer, and then a deep, booming voice came on.

"Ms. Dixxon, Paul Justin here."

"Good morning, Mr. Justin. To what do I owe the pleasure of speaking with you today?"

"Please, call me Paul." When Taylour didn't reciprocate, he continued, "We, uh, need to talk. Is now a good time?"

"Certainly, Paul. What would you like to talk about?"

The Fallen Body

"It seems that new evidence has been uncovered in the investigation of the murder of Neal Baines. And, while it does not completely exonerate your client, Ms. Sarah Baines, we are entertaining the notion of dropping the charges against her."

Taylour gasped audibly, and her eyes opened wide. There was an implied follow up to that statement, so she said, "And?"

The DA cleared his throat. "If we drop the charges, we would expect your client to tell us everything she knows. About what happened that night, what she knows about her husband and his, er, affairs, his work. Everything."

"And what happens if you don't get the answers you are looking for?"

"Ms. Dixxon, please understand that we may have, uh, jumped the gun a bit in arresting your client without all of the facts." Taylour could almost smell the sweat on his brow through the phone.

Taylour sensed an opening and couldn't help but exploit that bit of information, so she dug the knife in a bit. "Why did you arrest my client, Paul? Why not just take her in for questioning? I mean, she clearly wasn't strong enough to toss the body over the side. Even if she had had an accomplice, the testimony of the doorman states that he did not witness her going to Mr. Baines' apartment, let alone with someone."

"We looked at the fact that she fled the scene and became a fugitive as a sign of a guilty conscience, so naturally we thought she had something to do with Mr. Baines' demise."

"Did it even occur to your team that she might have had a legitimate reason to come to Marlinsville, say, to deal with a property that she recently inherited? While leaving the scene may look suspicious to you, from my perspective, my client may simply have been scared. Her choice to come to Marlinsville would not only allow her to lay low for a while, but also to take care of her aunt's affairs at the same time."

A longer pause this time. Taylour was enjoying Mr. Justin's discomfort a little too much, so she offered a gesture of good will. "I will be happy to talk with my client and encourage her to tell you what she knows, within reason."

Taylour heard an audible sigh of relief on the other line. "Certainly, within reason." Trying to salvage some of his dignity, he continued, "If she cooperates, we will drop all charges. But, if we find that she has not told the truth in order to protect herself, all bets are off. Understood?"

"Understood." Taylour pumped her fist in the air.

"Let me have my secretary schedule some time on my calendar. Hold on."

Taylour could hear Mr. Justin yell to Evelyn, his secretary, to come into his office, and then heard him give her instructions.

When she heard Evelyn pick up the phone, Taylour said, "I am on my way to your office and will be there by 11 a.m. this morning. I am sure that your boss will be happy to see us then."

"Why certainly, Ms. Dixxon. 11 o'clock is perfect." She gave Taylour directions and Taylour jotted them down, and then thanked her and hung up.

Another clang of the bell over the front door. Taylour let out a whoop and did a little dance while saying out loud, "I did it / I did it / I got my client o-off!"

Betty poked her head in and was immediately given a celebratory hug by her boss. After Taylour explained

The Fallen Body

what had just transpired, Betty let out a whoop of her own.

"We did it / We did it / We showed the Man who's bo-oss!" After singing this a few time in unison, they both fell to the ground in giggles.

Chapter 12

Mr. Justin couldn't put the phone down quick enough after talking with Taylour. That woman made him nervous, and it wasn't over yet. He heard Evelyn say 11 o'clock would be perfect, so he pushed aside the headache that he felt coming on and contacted his Assistant District Attorney, Jake Stedman, who had argued on behalf of the county at Ms. Baines' bond hearing. After reaching Mr. Stedman, the DA gave orders to his ADA so that he could arrange for Sarah to be in his office at the appointed time.

Another one of his ADA's popped her head in to ask a question, so Mr. Justin dropped off with Mr. Stedman. The young ADA bantered back and forth with her boss for a few minutes. She acted as the prosecutor in a high stakes burglary case about which she had questions, while he played devil's advocate. They did this for a few minutes until Evelyn rang him on the intercom. It was Jake Stedman again, and he sounded frantic.

"Jake, what's up?"

"Uh, boss, we have a problem. Ms. Baines' was assaulted last night."

The Fallen Body

"What?" The DA sat stiffly in his chair and started rubbing his eyebrow. "How did this happen? And why are we just hearing about this now?"

"Er, the details are still a little sketchy, but she seems to be OK. Just some bumps and bruises. As to why we weren't notified, the sheriff has been on vacation and just returned this morning. Sounds like his number two dropped the ball somehow."

The DA shook his head, sighed, and then asked, "Did they notify Ms. Baines' attorney?"

"I asked, and the sheriff's administrative assistant couldn't give me a straight answer. Believe me, I laid into them, but I don't think she cared one way or the other about how I felt about it."

Mr. Justin thanked his ADA and hung up. He weighed calling Ms. Dixxon again, but then decided that this was best addressed when she got to his office later that morning. He was going to make sure that the sheriff himself delivered Ms. Baines' personally to his office.

He made one more call, got a positive response to his inquiry, and then breathed a sigh of relief. Maybe this was not going to be so bad after all.

Chapter 13

Sarah opened her eyes when she heard the metallic clanging, temporarily disoriented as to her surroundings. When she lifted herself off of the thin mattress of her bottom bunk, her muscles screamed in agony, and she collapsed back down. Her eyes grew moist as the pain took over. She found that if she didn't move, the sharpness in her body would gradually subside to a dull ache, but it was impossible for her to stay motionless as she needed to go to the bathroom. She twisted her head around so that she could see the stainless steel bowl that was her toilet. She focused her gaze on it as she slowly rose. If she could stare at it, really stare at it, she might be able to push the pain aside. Her vision narrowed as she staggered forward and she almost blacked out, but she was determined, so Sarah took one step after another until she reached her destination.

After Sarah finished, she limped over to the small sink, splashed some water on her brow and cheeks, and winced at the image staring back at her from the small mirror that was bolted to the wall. Tangled hair, a bloody, swollen lip and one black eye, not to mention the bruises up and down both her thighs and forearms. Luckily those marks were hidden from the casual observer by her bright orange jumpsuit that was three sizes too big. Not her finest moment.

As she sat on the lower bunk, Sarah turned her mind over to some self-retrospection. She did not like making decisions for herself. She had always been the one to follow what others told her to do. That was why she and Neal had been such a great fit. He saw her innocence and felt like he needed to protect her, and she wanted to feel taken care of. Other women saw her as young and inexperienced, and maybe she was.

She glanced down at her fingers. Her friends often commented on how long and delicate they were, and she took great pride in making sure they were well manicured. Just one of the many perks of marrying into money. Holding them up to the faint light in her cell, both of her hands had numerous chips and scrapes now, and the color had long since faded from the harsh soap that she was forced to use.

When she fled to Marlinsville, she struggled with taking care of herself. Buying groceries, taking care of a yard, those were all foreign tasks to her. While she liked children, it was probably a good thing that she and Neal didn't have any. Kids would have been too much of a burden on her carefree lifestyle. Also, her parents were getting old and, while she had her sister, she had no other family to speak of.

"Sarah Cockrell Baines!" Sarah jerked her head up at the mention of her name and saw two guards on the outside of her cell. One spoke into his walkie talkie on his left shoulder, and then there was a loud click as the door unlatched and slid open.

"Hands out."

Sarah complied.

The Fallen Body

"Feet together." The guards attached cuffs on her wrists and ankles, the thick silvery chain clinking as it brushed against her jump suit. The guards each grabbed an elbow and slowly guided Sarah through several metal gates until they arrived at the conference room next to the sheriff's office.

The sheriff came into the conference room through a side door and apologized for making her wait. He sat down next to her, asked her if she was OK – she nodded that she was—and then expressed his deepest sorrows for what had happened to Sarah. He told her that he had disciplined the perpetrator of her assault and gave Sarah assurances that her attacker would be taken care of appropriately. The only thing that she could manage was the occasional nodding or shaking of the head as the sheriff offered his apologies again and again.

Finally, he rose from his seat. "Ms. Baines, please follow me."

"Why? Wh-where are we going?" Sarah said in a croaked whisper.

"We are going to see the District Attorney."

"Is there something wrong? Don't I have a right to speak with my attorney?"

The sheriff shook his head. "She will be there."

Sarah, resigned to her fate, said nothing more.

Chapter 14

Taylour arrived at the DA's office at precisely 10:57 a.m. and was quickly ushered into a side conference room by Evelyn. She declined Evelyn's offer for coffee, tea, or water, and then sat down. Evelyn disappeared into the DA's office to let him know that Ms. Dixxon had arrived. He immediately came into the conference room, followed by Mr. Stedman, and they both greeted Ms. Dixxon with firm handshakes, which she returned.

"Your client should be here any minute, Ms. Dixxon."

"Please, call me Taylour. I appreciate you meeting me on such short notice."

"Uh, certainly, Taylour. We understand how hard this has been on your client, so we are very interested in hearing what she has to say."

There was an awkward pause as they waited. The DA looked at his watch and grimaced. He sat down opposite of Taylour, made a motion with his head towards his ADA, who left in a hurry, and tried to make small talk.

"So, how was your trip up from, er, uh…"

The Fallen Body

"Marlinsville? It was uneventful." Taylour was not going to make this easy for him, but at the same time, she didn't want to create an unnecessary enemy, so she asked about his family. He responded more confidently, discussing their latest vacation that they had taken to Orlando. The DA had three kids, all teenagers, and they were all busy with school and band and football. He lamented not being able to spend as much time with them as he would have liked, and Taylour half listened to his responses to her questions while they waited.

Mr. Justin glanced at his watch in annoyance, which read 11:13 a.m., apologized for the wait, and fidgeted in his seat.

At 11:20 Jake finally came back to the room and announced that the sheriff had just arrived with Sarah. He remained standing until the sheriff entered the room with Sarah, who was still in her bright orange jump suit.

Taylour's initial smile at Sarah immediately changed when she saw that Sarah had a black eye.

"Oh my! Sarah, what happened?" Not waiting for a response, she turned to the sheriff. "Sheriff?"

He tried to look at Taylour, but found it difficult as he apologized. "I accept full responsibility for what happened, Ms. Dixxon. Ms. Baines' was attacked by one of the inmates last night, and—"

"Last night? When last night?"

"Uh, it was around 9:50 p.m. Just before lights out."

Taylour turned to the DA, who was squirming in his chair. "Why didn't you tell me this when we talked this morning?" She pounded her fist on the table.

"Taylour, listen, I—"

"That's Ms. Dixxon to you, sir."

The Fallen Body

The DA cleared his throat. "I, myself, did not hear about this, er, attack until this morning, after our conversation."

"Mr. Justin, I don't know what kind of game you are playing here, but an assault of my client while in *your* custody is a very serious matter." Her eyes swept the room, and no one dared look at her directly.

She softened her stare as she turned to her client. "Sarah, are you OK?"

Sarah nodded her head. "I'm OK. Just some bumps and bruises." Her stare was without emotion, which Taylour interpreted as shock. Taylour reached out to take Sarah's hand, which seemed to break Sarah's reverie, and she turned the corners of her mouth up a bit.

"Mr. Justin, I demand that my client be taken to the hospital to be cared for. Considering the shock that she has just been through, I ask that we postpone this interrogation until she has healed."

The sheriff spoke up. "Ms. Dixxon, Sarah has already been to our infirmary last night and has been treated. They took X-rays and found no broken bones, thankfully. She has a few bruised ribs, some minor cuts and abrasions, but nothing serious."

"Sheriff, I consider this to be *very* serious, even if you don't."

Sarah said, "Taylour, I appreciate your concerns, but everything is fine. I-I want to do this now."

Taylour frowned, twirling her pencil in her hand. "OK. Although it is against my better judgment, if my client wants to proceed, then let's proceed."

Those in the room all sighed with relief, and the tension dissipated considerably. Everyone took their seats and the District Attorney started.

The Fallen Body

"Sarah, I want to express my deepest apologies for putting you through this. While I don't feel it is required to explain why we initially focused our attentions on you, I did want to tell you that in doing some follow-up work, the police found some additional evidence that was missed previously." He sighed, pinched the bridge of his nose, and then continued. "I don't feel it appropriate to divulge that evidence at this time. Suffice it to say that we feel that, in the best interests of justice, we are going to drop all charges against you for the murder of your husband."

Sarah looked puzzled. "Do you mean, I'm free?"

"Yes, you are free to go."

A huge smile broke out on Sarah's face, and suddenly she was hugging Taylour and weeping on her shoulder. "I don't know how you did it, but thank you!"

Taylour hugged her back and said, "It wasn't me. This is all the DA's doing."

Sarah let go of Taylour and turned to the DA. "Thank you!"

The DA, as tough as he was, appeared touched by this sudden and genuine outburst of emotion. He smiled at Sarah and said, "You're welcome, Ms. Baines. My deepest condolences on the loss of your husband, Neal."

At the mention of her husband's name, Sarah wept again. The men in the room exchanged glances and sat awkwardly, not knowing what to say. Just then, a new figure entered the room. The DA stood up, welcomed Philip Davidson, and then introduced him to those around the table. Taylour eyes locked onto Philip, who gave her an amused, half smile from her shocked expression. She blushed and looked away.

"Mr. Justin, may I ask why he is here?" Taylour said as she gestured towards Philip.

The Fallen Body

Appearing like he finally had the upper hand, the DA said, "I will explain his reason for being here in a moment, Ms. Dixxon." Turning to Sarah, he asked, "Now, Ms. Baines', your attorney and I have discussed this moment earlier. In exchange for dropping the charges against you, we would, er, humbly ask that you tell us everything that you know about your husband, including your involvement the, ah, unfortunate night that he passed." He studied her closely and clasped his hands together expectantly.

Sarah sniffed and nodded. "I can do that."

"Thank you. Please, proceed."

Her voice was soft as Sarah went over the events of that night. She seemed embarrassed about how she snuck in without the doorman noticing her. Sarah described the feelings that she had as she went up the elevator, as well as her determination when she knocked on the door.

"He seemed surprised to see me, but he quickly recovered as he let me in."

She then described how she hid the gun behind her, and then only pointed it at him when she noticed the candles lit on the table. When she told of how he had Harry Connick, Jr. on in the background, more than a few of them chuckled. The entire room was centered on Sarah as she continued, a little more confident than before.

Sarah illustrated how she held the gun towards her husband, and then tried as best as she could to explain the emotions that she felt as he seemingly talked his way out of being gunned down by her. She described her hesitancy and how his promises that they would talk about their relationship after he met with his client made her feel like he really did love her and he wanted to work things out and she just wanted to believe him and so she left, hoping that they could work it all out. Her words spilled out at the end, and everyone sat there, with questions of their own that they wanted to ask.

It was Taylour who broke the silence. "Sarah, can you tell us about what you did with the gun?"

Everyone's number one question was about the gun, so they each leaned in to hear her response.

At first, she hesitated, and then she said, "Well, to tell you the truth, I had forgotten all about the gun. I must have put it into my bag before leaving the apartment." She scrunched up her face as if trying to remember. "All that I can remember is that when I exited the building, I reached into my purse to get the car keys. When I touched it – the gun, I mean – I pulled my hand back suddenly. I was shocked to realize that I had waved it at him and that I almost went through with it. I wanted nothing more to do with that thing, so I saw a garbage can and practically threw it in. To me, it was like poison and I wanted it as far away from me as possible."

Taylour thanked her for explaining that point. The rest in the room took turns asking Sarah questions, which she answered with poise, confidence, and grace. After ninety minutes of back and forth, the DA looked around the room and saw that no one had any more questions, so he thanked her for her cooperation. He was just about to turn the meeting over to Mr. Stedman when Philip cleared his throat. The DA slapped his hand to his forehead.

"Sorry, I almost forgot another important matter, one that required Mr. Davidson to attend." He extended his arm towards Philip, who had remained quiet throughout the meeting. "I have invited Philip Davidson of the Texas Rangers to this meeting because we both agree on one vital point." The DA turned to Sarah.

The Fallen Body

"Ms. Baines, we believe you to be in grave danger." He paused to allow those words to sink in. "Mr. Davidson has agreed to head a team of Texas Rangers to protect you."

Sarah and Taylour looked at each other. Taylour, taken aback, spoke first. "Um, OK. This is an interesting turn of events. May I consult privately with my client?"

"Certainly. I am going to leave you in Mr. Davidson's capable hands as I have a pressing engagement at one o'clock. So, if you will excuse me…" The DA left and everyone else followed him out.

Sarah sat back in her chair, exhausted from her interrogation, and said, "Grave danger? What does he mean by that?"

"He means that the attack yesterday may be from someone trying to silence you. At the very least, they may be trying to send you a message that if you talk, you'll be sorry."

"It seems kind of late for that, don't you think?"

"Yes, it does. However, we have to think that the attack on you was not random. We have to operate under the assumption that someone may be trying to hurt you."

"But I don't want to be a fugitive, Taylour! I just want things to go back to the way that they were before all of this happened."

Taylour took a hold of Sarah's hand and said, "Things are never going to be the same for you, from this point on."

Chapter 15

After Mr. Davidson was invited back in, he discussed the details of protective custody with the two of them.

"So, you think protective custody is my best option?" Sarah asked Taylour.

"I do. Philip is going to take you to a safe house that is within an hour of Marlinsville. He and some of his Texas Ranger colleagues will take good care of you."

The DA mentioned in their earlier meeting that Hon. Sherrie McMann felt it prudent to keep Sarah under watchful supervision, just in case.

Taylour told Sarah that she felt it necessary to limit her contact with Sarah through Philip only, so if there was any attempts to trace or track Sarah through Taylour, those attempts would be more easily thwarted. It certainly wasn't fool-proof, but under the limited timeframe that they had to plan, they didn't have many other options. Taylour made arrangements to pack up the essentials that Sarah would need from her house in Marlinsville and then deliver them to Philip once Sarah was settled later that evening.

The Fallen Body

After making the final arrangements for Sarah's release, which included changing her clothes out of the jail's jumpsuit, Philip and Sarah headed south out of downtown Dallas to the undisclosed location. As they chatted politely, Sarah noticed that small talk did not come easy for Philip, maybe because it required divulging too much about himself. Sarah, on the other hand, found herself telling stories about herself that she had never told anyone else. She did most of the talking as they zoomed down the road, passing farm after farm. While the interstate offered a more direct route to their destination, it did little in the way of scenery. The two of them didn't seem to mind, however.

After a few hours, Philip exited the interstate and wound his way through a number of small towns, each more rural than the next. There were red oaks and maples that dotted the flat landscape, but otherwise it was prairie grass for miles and miles. Dark clouds were forming to the west, but they were still too far away to threaten the stillness that had settled over the area.

They rolled to a stop at a quaint ranch house that was perched at the top of a hill. As Sarah got out, she took a long, deep breath of fresh air through her nose. She smelled cut hay and a faint hint of manure. Just enough to remind her that she was not in the city any longer. A slight breeze caused her to grab her arms from the chill, so she hurried her steps to the front porch and turned her back towards the wind, which had picked up slightly.

"Storm coming in," said Philip, who was carrying his bag and a few things for Sarah. He took out a set of keys, opened the heavy oak door, and let her go in first.

The smell of pine assailed her as she stepped into the large, dark room, her hand searching against the wood

The Fallen Body

panel wall for the light switch. After a few seconds she found it and turned it on. The place looked like it had been designed by a modern Jedediah Smith, with a bison head mounted over a dark brown leather couch in the living area, a solid oak table and four slatted chairs in the dining area, and a kitchen and sink in the far back corner. She turned and found a wood burning stove against the wall and the stove pipe that went up through the ceiling, dispersing its heat from its central location. A short, narrow hallway led to the bedrooms and a full bathroom, so she turned and wandered in that direction. The entire floor was wood, a blend of light and dark brown cedar that creaked slightly as she entered the hall. She admired the oil paintings on the walls, the crimson vistas of sandstone jutting from the desert floor, with sagebrush and vibrant blue, cloudless skies.

Sarah turned to the right and entered what appeared to be the smaller bedroom. Philip called to her and she turned to see him without her things.

"I'll take this room so that you can have the larger one. It offers you more privacy," Philip said. He pushed past her and dropped his bag, and then led her to her bedroom. The room was decorated in desert colors, with the canopy bed raised high off the floor and the throw pillows arrayed on the thick comforter.

It was all so warm and inviting, the feeling of comfort and peace in stark contrast to the harshness and sterility of the county jail, that Sarah leaned against the bed and let the tears come.

"Er, I'm sorry about all of this, Ms. Baines'." Philip shuffled his feet as he stood in the doorway.

"Please, call me Sarah." She sniffed and reached for a tissue that was on the nightstand. "I-I apologize for being so weepy. It just feels good to be here."

The Fallen Body

She smiled at Philip's discomfort, and he chuckled as he looked at her. "You hungry?"

"I'm starving! But I wanted to clean up first."

Philip nodded his head and closed the door behind him.

She longed for a warm shower, to close her eyes and let it cleanse her from head to toe. As she opened the opaque door, she was delighted to see liquid soap instead of a bar. She stayed under the water until it gradually turned cold. When she was done, Sarah dried herself off and put on a plush cotton bathrobe for the first time in what seemed like forever. She opened up drawers, searching for a brush to run through her hair. Finding only a men's black comb, she stood in front of the mirror and passed it through her thick hair. While the progress that she made was slow, if she used the thicker part of the comb, she was able to get out most of her tangles.

Sarah sat on the end of the bed and stroked the comb through her hair. She found herself fighting to stay away, so she quickly changed into clean clothes, and then walked into the kitchen. The aroma of freshly baking potatoes hung in the air, and she heard the crackle of grease as the fried chicken cooked on the stove. Sarah stood just out of Philip's view and watched his movements as he turned the chicken to keep it from burning, and then removed the casserole so that it could cool. She felt a pang in her heart that he had gone to so much trouble.

Finally, Sarah entered the kitchen. "That smells delicious!" Seeing that the table had not yet been set, she went to the cupboard and grabbed some plates and glasses.

The Fallen Body

"Thank you, Ms. Baines', er, Sarah. I don't get many opportunities to show off my culinary skills, so I hope you like it."

Sarah blushed as she set the table. She remembered a time with Neal where he had come home early from work and had made her dinner as a surprise. Oh, how she missed him!

She sauntered over to the refrigerator and asked what Philip would like to drink. When he said water, she pulled out two bottles and placed them on the table, and then turned abruptly to get ice.

"Whoops!" she said as she bumped into Philip, who almost dropped the potatoes. Their bodies met and Sarah blushed again. "I am so sorry! I-I didn't mean to..."

"It's OK, no harm done." Philip managed to step aside and place the food on the table.

"Uh, let me get a hot plate for that," said Sarah. She hurried over to the other side of the kitchen and started opening up drawer after drawer, searching, but not finding what she was looking for. She slammed the last drawer shut and stood there, alone, and a wave of emotion hit her. The dissonance of her former life with Neal and this new, artificial life was causing all kinds of confusion. She fought back the tears as she turned to face Philip.

"I-I don't know what came over me. I-I'm sorry for being so emotional."

Philip was frozen, still holding the casserole dish. He looked to Sarah with his head half-cocked, and then he softened his expression in understanding. He placed the dish down and went over to Sarah.

"Sarah, you don't need to apologize. I get it."

The Fallen Body

Sarah threw her arms around him, pulled him tight, and cried into his shoulder. He hesitated for a moment, and then awkwardly hugged her back.

Ring! The sound of the wall phone broke through, and the two of them separated. Philip went to the phone, spoke into it for a few moments, and then hung up. Meanwhile, Sarah sat down at the table and waited for Philip to complete his call.

"That was Ms. Dixxon, er, Taylour. She went to your place in Marlinsville to get some things for you."

Sarah nodded. "Is she coming here?"

"Ah, no, it's best for your safety to keep private visits to a minimum, at least for a few weeks. I've arranged to meet her tonight to get your stuff."

Sarah sighed and nodded again. Adjusting to her regular routine was not going to be easy.

On to a different topic, something that she had been pondering about since her husband was murdered. "Philip, I have a business matter that I wish to discuss with you."

Chapter 16

Roman entered the cabana huffing from his eight mile jog along the beach. Walking through his bedroom to the bathroom, he removed his clothes and stepped his 6'2" frame into the shower. The water cooled him down as he wiped away the sweat and sand. After drying off and putting on a thin, cotton bathrobe, he booted up his computer. He went straight to his offshore bank's website, signed in, and checked his bank balance.

The cries of the seagulls mixed with the lapping of the waves on the isolated Barbados shoreline. The palm trees swayed up and down and their sharp needle-like leaves rustled as a slight wind blew off of the deep emerald waters. The luxurious cabana was situated in the shade at the top of the sand berm, with the doors and windows open to allow the salty smell of the ocean to pass through.

This is where Roman Danshov preferred to come every Thanksgiving holiday week, away from the crowds, before going back to the controlled chaos of New York City, the city that never slept. He had made it a part of his routine, a place where he could decompress and clear his mind. It made him more effective, and more lethal.

The Fallen Body

He browsed the major newspaper websites, and this time he including the Dallas Morning News in his perusing, but saw nothing of interest. He had followed the online news right after he killed Mr. Baines, but then he had to wait several weeks for the announcement of her capture. He had finally breathed a sigh of relief when the bylines splashed a picture of Sarah Cockrell Baines all over the Internet and announced that she had been found and arrested for the murder of Neal Baines. The plan was falling into place.

While he didn't think that the police would find anything on him, he thought that killing Mr. Baines with the gun that Ms. Baines brought would have the desired effect, which was to focus the efforts of law enforcement away from him. Even if they finally realized that she didn't murder him and looked for someone else, the trail would have gone cold. He was not planning on visiting Dallas any time soon.

Roman was just about to shut down his browser when he saw the headline "Suspect in Murder of NJ man Released." As he read the article, he cursed under his breath.

> In an extraordinary move, Dallas police released Sarah Cockrell Baines from custody earlier this month. Baines, 38, had been accused of murdering her husband after he fell twenty stories from the exclusive downtown Dallas apartments, The Tower Residences, on Oct. 2. According to sources in the Dallas District Attorney's office, additional evidence was uncovered that exonerated Baines from having participated in the crime. Police do not

have any additional suspects at this time, but they continue to investigate.

Neither Baines nor her attorney was immediately available for comment.

Roman re-read the part that said that additional evidence was uncovered. What additional evidence? What, if anything, did Sarah tell them? And what does it mean that they do not have any additional suspects? Does that mean that they do not have any suspects, or that they do not want anyone to know that they do have suspects, but are not willing to say to the press who they are?

More cursing as he started to pace the room, clenching and unclenching his fists. He had been so careful not to be seen. He went over and over in his mind the events of that night and could not come up with how the police might have any additional evidence. He was not seen by anyone, and he made sure that he exited the building from the back. The camera on the 20th floor pointed away from the stairs that he took, and towards--.

He stopped suddenly, and then went back to his computer. He searched for the website to The Tower Residences, found it, and started going through their picture gallery.

Bam! He slammed his fist on the table. Staring back at him was a picture of the elevator bay on one of the floors, with a large mirror placed on the wall. The ornate frame was unmistakable. Based on what he knew about the security camera and how it was positioned, he surmised that someone standing in the opposite alcove could be seen in the mirror. That meant that he could have been seen in the security footage.

The Fallen Body

Roman rubbed his chin in thought. He still had time to slip away to an undisclosed location, but he did not want that type of a life. The life of a fugitive. Always having to look over his shoulder. Never being able to truly relax knowing that someone, somewhere, could come for him. He had been so careful up to this point, especially since his release from prison where he spent 10 years of his life atoning for a previous mistake. A mistake that he did not want to repeat.

He needed answers, so he decided to book the next flight to Dallas, Texas, which had a layover in Miami where he would stay overnight. He needed background information in a hurry, so he made a few phone calls and arranged for a package to be delivered to his hotel.

After getting off the plane and retrieving the package in Miami, Roman booked a room in a non-descript hotel close to the airport. He went over the package contents and memorized the details, names, dates, and faces that he had been given. He paused to stare at a recent driver's license photo of Taylour Dixxon, Sarah's attorney. While driver's license photos are almost never flattering, this one captured a few characteristics that Roman noted with interest. Strong, yet feminine. Determined, yet soft. Intelligent, but not in a nerdy, geeky, sort of way.

He needed to find Sarah, and if Sarah was going to be in protective custody, Taylour Dixxon was going to be the key to finding her. He did not relish the thought of having to kill Ms. Dixxon -- there was something about her that struck at his heart -- but he would if he had to. For him, the completion of the mission was paramount. The only thing that could stop him from accomplishing his assigned task was if he was dead.

He did not want to die.

Chapter 17

Taylour went to Sarah's house, located the key under the flower pot by the porch door, and let herself in. There was a faint smell of Ben-Gay and sulfur, and the decor was definitely 1960's, with bright pink shag carpet and color combinations of turquoise and green on the wallpaper and furniture. There were a few empty boxes leaned up against the planter box, with a tape dispenser and a couple of Sharpie markers. All of her house plants were in various stages of distress, from her Philodendrons and Spider plants to her English Ivy, so she looked in the cupboard for a cup to water them all. After that task, she made her way into the master bedroom.

Taylour spotted some suitcases in the closet, so she pulled those out and started packing them full of clothes. She found a smaller bag and loaded up items from the vanity in the bathroom. She noticed that the linoleum was worn and bubbled in spots, and the tile and porcelain surfaces were dusty, so she searched for a feather duster in the hall closet and went to work.

She thought about how difficult it must be for Sarah, with the loss of her husband and then to be accused of murdering him. Taylour had sensed in Sarah a sadness

The Fallen Body

that ran deep, almost as if happiness eluded her. Had she been in love with Neal? Or did she simply marry him so that she could have someone take care of her? She sensed that Sarah was carefree and not easy to pin down, so a commitment to marriage seemed hard to believe.

After she finished fixing the place up, Taylour hauled the suitcases and bags to her car and put them in her trunk. She glanced at her watch and called Philip to arrange for him to pick up the things that she had gathered up for Sarah. They agreed to meet at 11 p.m. at the Tom Thumb parking lot of the next town over.

Taylour pulled into the mostly abandoned parking lot of the Tom Thumb and turned off her headlights to her car, but kept it running so that she could stay warm. She turned to see if she could spot Philip's vehicle, a silver Ford Explorer, but he was not there yet. She glanced at her watch, which said 11:08 p.m. He was late.

At 11:10 that night, a silver Ford Explorer pulled up next to her, so she got out of her warm car and popped the trunk open.

"Mr. Davidson, nice of you to show up."

"Please, call me Philip." He smiled at her, but she was wary.

"What?" she asked.

"Oh, I don't know. I guess I admire your loyalty to your client."

Taylour softened a bit. "Thanks. I feel like I dodged a bullet, though."

"What do you mean, exactly?"

She shifted in her seat, and then turned to him. "Can you keep a secret?"

"Try me."

"Well, I've never tried a murder case before. It was starting to stress me out and I felt that I was neglecting my other clients. So, it is a bit of a relief to not have that hanging over me." Taylour exhaled, and then said, "The order of protection from the court was only for a short period of time. Do you really think Sarah is in danger?"

Philip rubbed his chin. "Hard to say. The attack that she suffered in jail could have been random, or it could have been sanctioned. Either way, it's smart to keep an eye on her for a while."

Philip turned to face Taylour. "So, you think you dodged a bullet, huh?"

"Yes, I do." She looked at him quizzically. "Do you know something that I don't know?"

Philip leaned into her a bit, his eyes wide open. "Sarah would like to hire us to find the real killer."

Taylour gave Philip an incredulous stare, and then sat back and stared forward. "I guess I didn't see that coming." She bit her bottom lip. "Does she know that we aren't private investigators?"

"Well, I have some accrued vacation that I could take, at least for a little bit. The pay would be decent, for both of us. I could use the contacts that I have to investigate and you could coordinate all the details."

Taylour's mind was whirling. "There is that. I have resources that I could tap into as well."

She turned again to him and noticed how close he was. His eyes were eager and dancing, as if he was a kid and had just been told that he was going to Disneyland.

She laughed. "OK, well then. I'll draw up the paperwork tomorrow and we can arrange for her to sign it."

"It's nice doing business with you, Taylour." He reached out his hand to shake hers, and she took it firmly.

"Likewise, *Philip*."

Chapter 18

After landing at Love Field, Roman hailed a taxi to take him to The Galleria in order to get some clothes. As the taxi headed north on the Dallas North Tollway, the driver asked, "So, where you from?"

Reaching into his pocket, Roman pulled out a money clip, squinted at the driver and peeled off a twenty. "I will give you a twenty now and another twenty at the end if you promise not to ask any questions, OK?" He folded it in half, lengthwise, handed the driver the bill, and the driver snatched it from Roman' hand.

"Sure thing! You won't hear another peep from me."

Roman settled back into his seat, closed his eyes, and tried to block out the stench of the driver's Old Spice cologne that wafted to the back seat. He tried to roll down the window, but for some reason, it didn't work. "Could you roll down the window back here? I need some air."

"Sorry, man, that window's busted. I've been fixin' to repair it, but I don't have the time. Man's gotta work."

Fixin' to repair it? What kind of English is this guy talking? Roman scrunched up his nose and scooted over to the other passenger window. He managed to get it down a few inches, which gave him some relief, but the roar of the air as they hurled down the road was deafening. *At least I do not have to talk with this joker.*

Roman shifted his left leg towards the center console to give himself some leg room. He hunched his head down to keep from rubbing the top of his head on the cab's interior, and then he shifted again to keep the door armrest from digging into his back. He tried closing his eyes again, but his awkward position in the back seat was putting a strain on his shoulders, so he settled his feet back down in front of him, which forced his knees into the back of the front passenger seat. *How did I get the smallest cab in this city?*

Meanwhile, the taxi driver had been whistling away as he maintained his speed at five miles under the speed limit.

Roman finally had enough. "You are killing me! The smell of your cologne, the broken window, the undersized back seat. And now you are whistling. What does a guy have to do to get some peace and quiet around here?"

"Jeez, man, lighten up. It's not like I--"

The cabbie froze as he felt the cold steel of the Colt Ace .22 caliber pressed against the side of his neck. "Hey, man, I don't want any troub--"

"I am not your ***man***. I just want to get to where I am going. I would consider it a favor to ***me*** if you would just get me to my destination, OK?"

The driver nodded. "We're cool, ma--, I mean, sir. Wh-whatever you say." The driver's hands started shaking, so he firmly grasped them on the steering wheel. Roman noticed beads of sweat form on the back of the driver's neck. He smiled and settled back into his seat. *Just have to show them who is the boss.*

The Fallen Body

The rest of the trip was uneventful. The taxi pulled up to the entrance of The Westin Hotel and the driver leapt out of the car to get Roman' bags that were in the trunk. Roman pulled out two 100-dollar bills and handed them to the driver without comment. The driver slammed the trunk closed, thanked Roman, and sped off, almost hitting two pedestrians on the way out of the roundabout.

Roman handed a twenty to the concierge after asking him to hold his bags for a few hours, and then Roman wandered through the lobby into The Galleria.

He walked to the center of the mall and looked down at the skating rink below. There was a huge evergreen in the center, decorated for the Christmas holiday, and kids circling round and round. There were young toddlers, with mom and dad on either side holding them up, as well as older children. They were all bundled up in thick coats, scarves, and mittens as they endlessly slipped along the icy surface.

Roman roamed around, peering into the different shops. This Black Friday promised to be hugely successful, with large sale banners hung in Christmas red and green, all shouting 20% Off, 30% Off, or Buy One, Get One Half Off. The aroma of Godiva chocolate combined with the smell of pizza coming from the Five Guys restaurant. Shoppers bumped into him as they passed, and some even muttered "Excuse me" as they held their bags in one hand and chattered on their cell phones with the other. The masses streaming past him reminded Roman of Grand Central Station, with the clickity, clackity of high heels.

He noticed a sign for Lucky Brand Jeans and strolled in. He motioned to one of the workers and passed him a twenty. The young man looked down at the bill as if he had struck gold, and said, "How may I--"

The Fallen Body

"I am looking for some jeans. I am going to be in the country, so I want something that will be able to withstand the elements, OK?"

"Sure, what kind of--"

"I want three of the relaxed fits. Dark."

"I'd be happy to get those for you. What are your--"

"My waist size is 38, and the length is 36."

"Great, let me get those for you." The shop clerk went over to the shelf and searched for three pairs that matched those measurements.

Meanwhile, Roman wandered over to the shirts and browsed the selections. He found a few plaid western shirts that suited his purposes, and then pulled a Schott down vest off the rack. He grabbed an Uttar beanie and a Donegal scarf, and then searched for shoes. Not finding any in the store, he caught the eye of the young man who was helping him, handed the items that he had already selected, and said, "I will be right back."

Roman marched over to the Carlo Pazolini store, bought a pair of brown and black suede boots, and carried those back to Lucky Brand Jeans.

The young man rang up his purchases, and was astonished when Roman handed him cash. "Would you like--"

"Walk out with me while I get a cab."

Roman strolled out and went back to The Westin. He asked the concierge for his bags and strode out to the first taxi in line. The young man from Lucky Brand Jeans hurried forward and put the packages in the trunk of the taxi. Roman handed him another twenty, and the young man thanked him profusely.

Before Roman got into the cab, he stuck his head in the window and sniffed. Not smelling anything too offensive, he opened the front passenger seat, moved it up as far as it would go, and then got in behind it. "Take me to the airport."

"Would that be Love Field? Or DFW?"

"I need to get a rental car."

"So, you want to go to the nearest rental car place?"

"Yes, I need to go quickly."

"Certainly." The taxi driver pointed to the Hertz Rent-a-Car that was just down the street from where they were.

Roman looked at the closed trunk where all of his packages were, then back at the driver. "Tell you what, you drive me over to the rental place, and I will make it worth your while, OK?"

"How much?"

Roman pulled out his money clip, peeled of another Benjamin, and said, "This enough?"

"Get in, I'll take you right now!" He rushed over to the passenger side and opened the door for Roman.

He got in, and the driver barely had a chance to ask any questions before they were in the Hertz parking lot.

"Wait here."

Roman went inside. Pointing at the black GMC Yukon, he said, "I want that one."

The woman at the counter looked up and asked, "Do you have a reservation, Mr. -- ?

"I do not have a reservation, but I would like to have that vehicle right there."

"I am happy to assist you, let me just get some information from you. Do you have a valid driver's license?"

Roman pulled out his license and passed it over.

"And which credit card would you like to put this on?"

"I will be paying cash for this, up front."

The Fallen Body

She cocked her head to one side and studied him more closely. "That is highly unusual, Mr. --"

"Danshov." He took his money clip and placed it on the counter. "I will pay cash for the rental, and I would also like to get the insurance policy."

She looked behind her, and then leaned over to him and whispered, "I'll make an exception in your case, Mr., er, Danshov." She reached for the money clip, and he placed his oversized hand on hers. She blushed visibly, but did not withdraw her hand. Roman felt the heat coming from her softness and wished that he had the time to explore his options, but he was on a time schedule and needed to get to his final destination.

He winked at her, grabbed the money clip from her grasp, and took ten 100 dollar bills out. *I might swing by here once the job is done.* "It has been my pleasure doing business with you." He followed her out, motioned to the cabby to start unloading and loading his suitcases and packages, paid him for his time, and then turned once again to the Hertz lady. As he reached for the keys, he held her hand up to his lips and kissed it gently. She blushed again and let her hand linger in his until he turned away. He winked at her one last time before getting into the car.

He sped away, finally on his way to Marlinsville, TX.

Chapter 19

Roman pulled into the Microtel at the top of the grassy, barren hill that overlooked Marlinsville, Texas. He opened his trunk, took his new jeans and shirts and packed them in his mostly empty suitcase. He grabbed a few of his other bags and sauntered up to the front desk. A woman, about 25 years old, Hispanic, greeted him, "Welcome to Marlinsville. How may I help you?"

"I need a room, non-smoking, at least for the next three weeks, with an option to stay longer. I will be paying cash." Roman pulled out his money clip and peeled off 15 one-hundred dollar bills. He handed them over.

Blushing, the clerk palmed the cash and leaned into him. "I've got just the room for you, Mr.--?"

"Johnson. Call me Jimmie." He chuckled at his little joke, and the woman laughed with him.

"Well, *Jimmie*, I have a room just down the hall on this main floor. Will Room 129 work for you?" When Roman nodded, she slid him his room key. Sizing him up, she continued, "We have a gym, also on this floor, through those doors just passed the elevator. We also have a complimentary continental breakfast bar between

The Fallen Body

the hours of 6 a.m. and 9 a.m. Here's a map of the town. I hope you enjoy your stay."

Roman nodded again and took his bags to his room. He opened the door and closed it tightly behind him, making sure to push the latch in place. He changed into his new clothes, and pulled out his weapons bag. Grabbing for the phone book, he made a note of where the courthouse was. He needed to reconnoiter, so he grabbed a pair of binoculars, the map, a note pad and a couple of pens, and placed them in a smaller bag. Placing the new cowboy hat on his head, he headed out the door. Since it was a nice afternoon out, not too chilly for the end of November, he decided to walk.

The Microtel faded in the distance as he wandered down the hill towards the downtown area. He passed a few strip malls, a bank, some stand-alone restaurants, and then turned the corner onto Oak Street. The area had just finished being renovated, and the sidewalks were bustling with people.

The aroma of salsa floated in the air, and Roman realized that he hadn't eaten since this morning, so he wandered over to Tortilla Casa. He asked for a table on the veranda, which was opened to accommodate the weekend crowd, and positioned himself so that he could observe.

A young couple, walking arm in arm, passed a few feet of where he sat, completely oblivious as they whispered to each other. The woman laughed at something her date said, and they continued on. An older gentleman, cowboy hat firmly on his head, ambled up to the door and held it open while a family of four exited, the mother telling her sons to stay close and to not wander out into the street while the boys flew their paper airplanes that their father had made from the kids menu.

The Fallen Body

Their father called to the boys to get over here, and they silently fell into line as they marched to their minivan. Another cowboy with his wife strolled past, and Roman caught a snippet of their conversation, something about the horses needing cleaner quarters and why doesn't Billy help and oh, he can't because he's busy with football practice.

The wind picked up a bit, and Roman wished that he had brought a jacket, but he suffered in silence. When the waiter came out, Roman ordered a chimichanga and lemonade. He silently ate his food after it was placed in front of him, paid the bill, and left. He wandered down the rest of Oak Street, passed the visitor's bureau, the city offices, an old fire station, and noticed field lights on at a softball field. Since he had nothing better to do, he strode over to watch.

It was a men's softball game, and the smell of dirt and popcorn mixed in what appeared to be a close game. The temperature was dropping fast, which seemed to add a sense of urgency in the players' movements. The home team was up six to three according to the scoreboard. The game was slow pitch, and the visiting team in red shirts was just about to take their turn at bat. It was the top of the 3rd inning. Shouts of "C'mon, Vernon, wait for your pitch," and "Who's up next?" and "Virgil, you're on deck" floated up to the stands.

The batter swung at a high, arching pitch. With a smack, he sent it deep to left field. The left fielder ran back, back, almost to the chain link fence, and then made a spectacular catch that was just inches from the top of the fence. Cheers from the small crowd rang out as the fielder threw the ball back into play. The shortstop caught the ball on one hop, pointed to the left fielder, and then tossed the ball to the pitcher. Two more long fly balls to left field and left center field respectively – and two more catches later – the home team returned to their dugout for their turn to bat. The white misty breath of the outfielders became more and more noticeable as the game progressed.

The left fielder took off her hat, shook her short, strawberry blonde hair out of her face, and then put her hat back on. Roman was surprised to see that the left fielder was a woman, so he watched her closely. When he saw the last name on her shirt, "Dixxon," he did a double-take. *Could this be?* Suddenly, the game had new meaning to him, so he settled in on the bleachers and peered more intently at her.

She moved with grace and confidence as she shouted encouragement to her teammates. They treated her as one of the guys, high-fiving her when they made a play and chiding her with boasts and playful taunts. When she went out to coach third base, she called plays, telling her runners what they should look for, and cheered them on as they rounded the bags towards home. When it was the home team's turn to field, someone tossed her mitt to her as she headed back out to left field.

The visiting team managed to tie the game up at seven apiece going into the bottom of the 6th inning. Roman saw Taylour Dixxon brandish a bat as she stepped up to the plate. She blooped one over the head of the second baseman and made it safely to first. The next batter swung hard, belting a fly ball to center field, which was caught. Taylour tagged up at first, and then sped to second, sliding in just under the throw. A cloud of dust flew up around the bag, and she grinned as she stood up and dusted herself off. One out. Taylour was in her element.

The Fallen Body

The next batter punched a one hopper to the shortstop, who fumbled picking it up, but he held Taylour to second base with a look towards the bag. Holding his throw to first, he tossed the ball to the pitcher.

The next batter grounded one to the second baseman, who managed to tag the runner, but was late in getting the throw to first, and Taylour advanced to third base. Two outs, with a runner on first and third.

The pitcher twirled the ball in his hand, checked Taylour at third, and then pitched the ball inside. The batter pulled the bat closer to his body and swung, hitting the ball almost on the handle. The ball dribbled slowly to the third baseman.

Taylour ran down the third baseline, passing the ball going the opposite direction just as the third baseman fielded it. Perhaps hoping to get the runner out, he made a quick decision to toss the ball to the catcher. The catcher stood up, blocked home plate, but had to step to the inside to get the line drive that missed Taylour's helmet by inches. He grabbed the ball out of the air and swung his arms to tag her out. The mitt caught her square in the left shoulder as she slid into home plate. There was a loud thump, followed by a scream of pain. Roman tasted the dust in his mouth as he waited for it to clear.

Taylour was writhing on the ground in pain, clutching her left shoulder. Her teammates rushed to her side, and someone called an ambulance. Heated words were exchanged between the pitcher of her team and the third baseman of the visiting team. The catcher was obviously shaken up as he hovered around the fallen base runner. "Are you OK, ma'am?"

The Fallen Body

Mesmerized at the scene before him, Roman was startled by the sound of sirens in the background. He left quickly. *I do not want any attention to myself.*

As he hustled back to his room on the other side of town, he smiled as he thought about what had just transpired. He shook his head in wonder. *She will make a formidable opponent. This may be harder than I thought.* He relished the idea of matching wits and brawn with Taylour Dixxon, legal counsel to Sarah Cockrell Baines.

Chapter 20

Sarah bolted upright in bed from her nightmare, a scream muffled in her throat. Her skin was clammy, her sheets and blankets disheveled as if she had been running. As the darkness of the early morning enveloped her reality, her breathing slowed to normal. She got out of bed and paddled to the bathroom to splash some water on her face.

The images in her dream had been so vivid and real. She remembered being in a large field dotted with large boulders, the sky filled with grey, swirling clouds. She held a large bronze shield on her left forearm and a double-edged sword in her right hand. A volley of arrows from an unseen enemy hidden in the trees darkened the sky, their deadly points zeroing in on her position. Neal was next to her, but he was unarmed and did not have a shield, so the two of them huddled together under hers.

They managed to survive the first wave of arrows, their points clinking harmlessly off the metal barrier Sarah had created for them. Once the arrows stopped, she feared that their position was about to be overrun, so she retreated back. However, Neal did not follow her as he was frozen with fear. She gestured frantically for him to get to where she was, but he wouldn't move.

"Neal, come over here! I can't protect you unless you come to me!" she cried out to him. When he refused to budge, instead of going back to him, she continued her retreat. Seconds later, she searched for him, and then screamed. Neal had two arrows protruding from his chest. He reached his hand out and asked, "Why did you leave me? Why?" He then fell to the ground, dead.

The coolness of the water was refreshing and helped the images slowly fade from her memory. She shuffled back to her room, got a robe to put on, and then decided to get some fresh air. As she opened the front door, a cool breeze picked up. She stared up into the starry sky and could barely make out the fuzziness of the Milky Way. The eastern sky was barely starting to lighten, the dawn still an hour away. Sarah walked barefoot on the porch, which extended to the two front corners of the ranch house. She could barely make out the fence line that divided the land from their neighbor's place, and noticed a barn down the road. The smell of hay was strong and lingered on her robe as she went back inside.

Instead of going back to bed, she decided to make breakfast. She flipped on the light in the kitchen and went to work. As she scrambled the eggs, her mind wandered over the nightmare that she had. The images were hard to remember, but the guilt was still very real.

Just as she finished making some toast, Philip wandered in, his eyes still half asleep. His short, gray hair was not too tussled, a sure sign of deep, worry-free sleep. Sarah automatically reached to fix her hair, combing it lightly with her fingers and pushing it behind her ears.

She smiled up at him and he smiled back. "Smells good."

The Fallen Body

"Thank you," Sarah said.

As they sat and ate in silence, she couldn't help but ask, "What are we going to do today?"

"Well, I was wondering if you wanted to get out a bit, maybe go to church. Nothing too fancy."

Sarah scrunched up her face. "Church? Well, I'm not exactly sure about that. I haven't been for a while."

Philip's eyes lit up. "It'll be good for you, a chance to reconnect with your spiritual side."

"OK, I'll go. But I don't have anything to wear."

Philip chuckled. "I remember carrying in several clothes that Taylour got for you from your house. I'm sure you can find something. We leave at ten." He went to get ready, a bemused smile on his face.

Sarah finished her breakfast and went to her room. She rummaged around her closet and settled on a deep violet Tout Sweep dress. Sarah laid it on her bed and went to fix her hair. Once she was done, she slipped her dress on over her head, adjusted her hair one more time, put on a pearl necklace and earrings, and then emerged from her room.

Philip stood up when she entered and gave her a quick smile. He was dressed in a white shirt and bolo tie, with a suit jacket draped over his shoulder.

In his best Southern drawl, he whistled and said, "Why, Ms. Baines, you are certain to turn some heads when we make an entrance!"

Sarah laughed for the first time in a long time, and then took his arm as they left. Philip helped her into the Explorer and then they drove off.

"I haven't dressed up like this in a while," Sarah said. She looked into the mirror from her sun visor and fussed with her hair.

The Fallen Body

Philip gave her a smirk and said, "You should do it more often. You look beautiful."

Blushing, Sarah said thanks. She folded her hands in her lap and watched the trees whiz by.

After ten minutes of driving, they pulled into a parking lot where other churchgoers were piling out. She noticed mothers and fathers carrying infant car seats and bags, while little children, dressed in their Sunday best, ran to pull open the door.

As Sarah went in, she felt a warm peace in her heart that almost knocked her over. It filled her entire body, from head to toe, and tears moistened her eyes. She gripped Philip's arm even tighter and smiled and shook hands with those that greeted them.

The soft organ music filtered back to where they were, at the back of the chapel, and she marveled at the happiness and calm that had come over her. Sarah could not remember ever feeling like she was at that moment. She held her breath, as if the very act of breathing would somehow cause the joy in her heart to dissipate. It was as if she had come home.

She glanced over at Philip and saw a glow on his face. She observed everyone else, and they also had the same glow. These people were happy to be here. That was not a sentiment with which she was familiar, as church-going as a child had always seemed like a duty to perform, something that you did because you were supposed to, not because you wanted to.

Just then, a man greeted Philip by giving him a bear hug, the two of them slapping each other on the backs.

"Sarah, this is my brother, Tom, and his wife, Jennifer, and their two kids, Alex and Aubrey."

Sarah smiled and politely shook hands with all of them, and then sat back down.

The Fallen Body

"Good to see you, bro!" Tom said.

"Yeah, I know. It's been a while."

The organ music stopped and the congregation suddenly got quiet as a man came to the microphone and started the meeting.

The man was tall and wore a dark suit, also wearing a white shirt and tie. He welcomed everyone, including visitors, and made a few announcements.

The congregation then sang a Christmas hymn, "Hark, the Herald Angels Sing," and then a prayer was said by a young woman. Sarah listened intently to the words, which were simple, yet powerful. Again, a wave of peace washed over her, and more tears ran down her cheeks.

Once the prayer was completed, more announcements were given, and then another hymn was sung in preparation for the sacrament.

A prayer was given over the sacrament, and then several teenage boys lined up to receive trays with pieces of bread that they then distributed to the congregation. Another prayer, then this time small cups of water were distributed. The entire passing of the sacrament took about ten minutes, and hardly a word or noise was made during that time. Even the small children sensed the solemnity of the moment and sat still, some of them with their arms folded.

Once the sacrament was completed, there were several short talks given by different members of the congregation, each one touching Sarah's heart in a different way. She laughed along with everyone else when one speaker recounted a story about how hard it was to get up every morning to go to something called seminary. She cried when another speaker talked about the recent death of her mother. Throughout the meeting, Sarah was frozen in place, not daring to move.

Finally, after a little more than an hour, a final hymn was sung and a prayer was given, this time by an older gentleman. As he prayed, he asked for a remission of sins to come upon those in attendance. Sarah's heart almost stopped, and she felt a familiar hardness settle in. Fear gripped her as if in a vise, and she could hardly breathe.

After everyone said "Amen," Sarah had the urge to flee. She whispered to Philip, "Can we go now?"

He stared at her, his head tilted, with pursed lips and nodded. They both said goodbye to Tom and his family, and then Sarah dragged Philip out. The wind picked up, blowing Sarah's hair in every direction. She quickly got in the Silverado and hung her head down.

"Is something wrong?" Philip asked.

Sarah stared at the glove compartment and shook her head. She turned to look out the window, hiding her face with her left hand as they slowly drove away.

Storm clouds billowed behind them as they tried to outrun the rain on their way back.

"Did you want to stop and get something to eat?" Philip asked.

Sarah shook her head, still unable to talk. The darkness outside mirrored her mood, almost as if a greater power was sending her a message.

A message of despair.

Chapter 21

The game of chess intrigued him. While he was no grand master, Roman was pretty good. He appreciated the possibilities of the different moves, the limitations of the movement of each piece, and the strategy needed to beat his opponent. At home in New York he had a habit of playing online until 2 or 3 a.m., which allowed him to stretch his concentration to its limits as he fought off fatigue. When he was faced with a particular challenge, it was not uncommon for him to go without food and water for hours on end as he fixated on knowing all the potential moves four or five turns ahead.

Tonight he had an important task to perform.

A dry, cold front had come through town, and the air was now frigid. Frost was appearing on the tops of the cars and on the windows in the Microtel parking lot. Roman, however, was not bothered by the cold. He looked at his watch, which said 11:37 p.m., and rubbed his hands together to get the blood circulating in his fingers. He opened up his rental car, threw his black working bag onto the passenger seat, and closed the door as quietly as he could. He didn't want to attract any attention to himself, tonight especially, since he was about to do something illegal.

He needed to record Taylour's conversations for any hints of a break in the case. In order to do that, he planned on breaking into Taylour's law office.

The roads through town were nearly empty as everyone else thought it wise to stay indoors, huddled under their blankets in front of their wood stoves or fireplaces. The chance of slipping on black ice deterred most people from going out, and the people in Marlinsville were no exception. Because of this, Roman was able to navigate his Yukon without anyone noticing where he was going.

Taylour's office was located on the end of a small strip mall at the top of a small hill on the opposite side of the town, which overlooked the rest of Marlinsville and the valley below. The word "hill" might be an overstatement. It was more of a rise, as Marlinsville was generally flat.

While driving through town Roman saw a few abandoned buildings with For Lease signs and phone numbers taped to the windows. As he came to a stop at the traffic light, he saw a Dairy Queen on the corner that was shuttered up for the winter. On the opposite corner he noticed that the Chevron gas station was still open, the bright neon red, white and blue casting a pall over the thickening coldness. Renovated retail store fronts appeared ahead of him, with names like Oak Street Candy, Emily's Emporium, and Central Texas Bookstore. Billie's Barbecue looked like it was a popular hangout, but not tonight as the building lights were turned off and the parking lot was bare. The streetlights gave off an eerie glow, but the darkness was never fully penetrated by their

The Fallen Body

luminescence, nor by the headlights of the Yukon as it made its way slowly down the town's main drag.

He passed the courthouse, which was on the left at the corner of Main Street and Pecan Avenue.

Finally, Roman turned into the parking lot in front of Taylour's office. He parked the car about fifty yards away from the door so as to not create any suspicion. As he crept to her door, he caught a glimpse of the gold-lettered sign on the glass door, which read: The Law Offices of Taylour Dixxon. The letters looked too fancy for the spartan surroundings. The other offices were vacant except for a bakery on the opposite end, which appeared to be closed for the weekend. The city cemetery was located just beyond the strip mall next to the office. The combined aroma of yeast and the smell of death pushed Roman to quicken his pace.

Just at that moment, the full moon broke through the clouds and illuminated the area. Roman pulled out his locksmith tools and went to work. His furtive glances found no threats, but the utter stillness in the air was disconcerting. When he finally released the door latch and made his way inside, he heaved a sigh of relief.

He wiped his brow, and then turned a penlight on, sweeping it from side to side so that he could understand the layout. He shown his light down the hall and walked slowly towards Taylour's private office. There were occasional reflections from the glass that covered different paintings along the wall, but otherwise the hall was bare.

He searched for an envelope that should have arrived in the mail this last week. He rummaged through the stack of papers, but did not find what he was searching for, so he headed down the hall.

The Fallen Body

As Roman approached Taylour's private office, he stiffened and went still. There was a soft whoosh of noise. Jerking his light around, he realized that the heating unit had turned on. Blowing out a quick breath, he turned back and reached for the doorknob.

He twisted it open and hurried inside. When he discovered that there were no windows in the office, he flipped the light switch. He winced a bit at the sudden illumination, but then he went to work.

Once he was done placing a bug in Taylour's phone, he placed another bug under her desk and out of reach. He grabbed his bag, went back to the front desk, and did the same thing with the main phone on Betty's desk. He also placed a bug under her desk, for a total of four bugs.

The hardest part now was finding a place for his wireless receiver that could be placed within range of his bugs and not easily detected. He looked up and down the walls, ceilings, and in the corners until he found exactly what he was looking for. The ceiling was tiled with removable pieces, each about 18 inches square, and held in place by upside down metal T-bars. These T-bars ran the width and length of the ceiling, which made it easy to push up on a tile, maneuver it sideways and diagonally so that it could be pulled down. Roman took out a tile from the hallway and placed it on the floor. He screwed a wireless receiver to the opposite, back side of the tile, flipped the electronic device's switch to the On position, and then replaced the tile back into the ceiling. The receiver operated on battery power that would last at least three months, which was more than enough time for Roman.

The bugs were each designed to transmit wirelessly to the receiver, which would then boost the audio conversations to the receiving device that Roman had attached to his PC back in his hotel room. The software that he had on his PC would then digitally capture the audio and compile it into different audio files, which would then be reviewed by Roman. The system was designed either to allow him real-time listening capabilities or to record the conversations and listen to them later.

Before Roman left, he glanced around to make sure that he didn't leave anything behind. Once he was satisfied, he gathered up his bag and headed for the door.

Suddenly, the headlights of a car swept the interior, and Roman dived for cover behind the wall. When the lights stopped right in front of Taylour's office, he slowly reached for his .22. He peeked around the corner and shielded his eyes from the light. While the blinds hanging from the window blocked most of the illumination, he could see through the door that someone was coming.

Breathing heavily, Roman heard an indecipherable, electronic chatter that came from the car, as well as the distinct sound of radio static. He jumped when he heard a deep human voice respond to the radio. More distinct radio static, and again, another human response, closer this time. The glaring headlights cast an oversized shadow of a man onto the front blinds as he sauntered slowly towards the front door of Taylour's office. In the darkness, Roman' hand clenched the butt of the gun as he raised it, pointing it directly at the dark figure on the other side of the door. His finger hovered over the trigger as he waited, waited, for the shape to come through the unlocked door.

However, just as the sheriff's deputy was about to place his hand on the door to check to see if it was locked, he paused, spoke again into his shoulder mike, and then retreated. The car turned on its red and blue

The Fallen Body

flashing lights and squealed out of the parking lot. Roman lowered his weapon and ran to the door. After watching the police car disappear into the cold night, he again let out a breath and sat down heavily in the receptionist's chair. *That was close! Too close.*

After a few minutes to allow his heart rate to come back to normal, Roman finally lifted himself up from where he was sitting and left the building, almost forgetting to lock it back up again. He glanced over at the cemetery and shivered, not from the cold, but from fear. He couldn't wait to get as far away from this place as possible.

Chapter 22

Taylour showed up at her office at 8 o'clock Monday morning wearing a sling, which cradled her left arm. She winced in pain as she pulled the door open with her good arm.

"What happened this time? Did you jump off a ledge trying to save a kitten from falling?"

Taylour scowled at Betty and said, "No, it was much more heroic than that. I scored the winning run in our softball game last night."

"You scored the winning run? Rumor has it you were out by a mile." Betty grinned up at her boss, handed her a file folder with a worn label that had become all too familiar, and continued. "You have a court appearance for the Larson case at 10 a.m. Everything you need is in that folder, including the petition to dismiss all charges."

Betty continued. "You still need to go over these land deeds that you promised to look at for the Grinwald estate. The executor is calling me every hour asking for you, and I can only hold them off for so long." Betty put on her reading glasses, which she had hanging from her neck on a silver chain that Taylour had given to her last

The Fallen Body

Christmas, and said, "But most importantly, you need to sign these checks. Today."

Taylour put her head in her right hand, winced again, and grabbed a pen from Betty's desk. She tapped the end of the pen on the desk, and then she signed her name. How quickly the money left as soon as it managed to come in. While she had a nice little practice going, she wasn't rich by any stretch of the imagination. Taylour put her head in her hands and wished that she was on a beach, taking in the sun – *who cares about skin cancer when you're my age* – with a good, beach book. It wasn't going to happen. Not while she worked for herself. Sigh.

"Maybe I can clone myself," she muttered.

"What was that?" Betty asked.

"Oh, nothing. It's just sad to see so much money leaving all at the same time. I don't know what I would do without you, Betty."

"You would shrivel up and die, is what you'd do. Someone would come in one day and find you in the fetal position over in the corner. You wouldn't be able to function--"

Taylour chuckled. "Yeah, yeah, you're indispensable. I get it."

"Just remember that when I come looking for a raise."

Taylour carried her work back into her office and sat down. Just as she was about to yell up to Betty for coffee, Betty yelled, "There is no coffee. You told me that you needed to wean yourself of that, so I replaced it with diet drinks, which are in the fridge in the break room."

Taylour walked across the hall, mumbling under her breath. She pulled open the refrigerator door and peered in. All she saw was Caffeine Free Diet Cokes. Sighing, she grabbed a can, placed it on the small break room table, and tried to pop the tab off with her one good hand. As she pulled up, the tab broke off, and the can skittered onto the floor. As it hit the corner of the cabinet, the small crack that she had managed to get burst open and spewed foam on the floor and the chairs with a sharp hiss.

"Aack! What a mess! Betty, can you please come in here?" Taylour held the damaged can over the sink until it stopped its sputtering, and yelled again for Betty.

Betty poked her head around the corner of the room and rolled her eyes. Shaking her head, she took the nearly empty can from Taylour's sticky fingers and threw the can into the wastebasket.

"Thank you, I owe you one," Taylour carefully fled back to her desk, taking care not to get any stickiness on the bottom of her velvet pumps. She promised herself that she would get some solid billable hours in. She managed to complete the work on the land deeds, making notes to give to Betty, and glanced at the clock on her desk. 9:30. Good, just enough time to go over the Larson case file before I need to head to the courthouse.

For the next ten minutes, she read the petition to dismiss all charges against her client, Mr. Barry Larson, who was being sued by his neighbor for building a fence on the property line that they shared. The complainant, Mr. Gerald Foster, was upset that the fence was not to his liking, but repeated attempts by Mr. Larson to get some kind of agreement to share the costs and the labor from Mr. Foster had gone unheeded, so Mr. Larson bought the materials, spent hours digging the holes for the fence posts, and placed the back side of the fence towards the Foster property.

Only after all the work was done did Mr. Foster complain to Mr. Larson. Words were exchanged, followed by even more heated emails, until finally Mr. Foster threatened to sue Mr. Larson for "creating an eyesore." All attempts at mediation had not produce a resolution that both could agree on, so that is why the matter was in the hands of the courts.

Chapter 23

"I'm not sure what to do, exactly." Taylour scrunched her face together.

"You have to decide." The voice on the other end was adamant.

"But I don't like my choices!"

"Ma'am, I'm sorry, but we need a decision."

"But you ran out of my favorite salsa de pebre. Frankly, the biggest reason why I buy your food is because of your salsa de pebre."

While Taylour was not a true Chili Head, which is a lover, collector and eater of hot chiles, right now she craved Tortilla Casa's salsa de pebre, or pepper sauce. After a long day at the office, she looked forward to having some carne asada, or grilled meat, smothered in salsa de pebre. It was usually made with jalapeños, but habaneros make it spicier.

Tortilla Casa was regionally famous for its different sauces, from their fruit salsas -- cherry, peach, pineapple, and mango -- to their ethnic salsas -- Chimichurri from Argentina and Uruguay, Guasacaca from Venezuela, Molho Malagueta from Brazil. They also featured their own Mexican salsa, Mole, and Queso, that brought people from miles around. Taylour was a frequent visitor, and like a lot of people, once she found something she liked, she stuck with it.

"We will be making some more this afternoon. You can try back then." Click.

Taylour grunted with displeasure, and then marched from her private office to the kitchen to see if there were any leftovers in the break room refrigerator.

"Betty, how old is this chimichanga?"

"I dunno. Is it growing any mold on it?"

Taylour pulled the plate out and peeled the tin foil back. It didn't smell too bad when she sniffed it, so she removed all of the tin foil and stuck it in the microwave for thirty seconds, and then pushed start. Once it was warmed to her satisfaction, she took it into her office and shoveled it down while she worked.

Taylour glanced again at her clock, which read 9:40, so she gathered up the Larson case file and headed out the door. Just as she went to push the door open, the phone rang and Betty answered it.

"Who may I ask is calling?" Pause. "Philip Davidson?"

Taylour shook her head, pointed to her cell phone, and walked out to her car. Knowing that she only had a few moments to spare, she decided to take her car instead of walking the few blocks to the courthouse.

She hated to waste so much time trying to find a parking spot, but she got lucky in her first pass through as there was an empty spot just ahead of her. She quickly pulled in, got out of her car, and was on her way through the courthouse doors when her phone rang.

"Hello?"

"This is Philip Davidson. We need to talk."

The Fallen Body

"Well, Philip Davidson, we do need to talk. Only now is not a good time. I'm just about to walk into court." Taylour placed her briefcase on the ramp for the X-ray machine to examine. "May I call you back in thirty minutes or so and arrange a time for us to chat?" She walked through the metal detector.

Beep, beep, beep.

"I would like that. But how about you put down your phone so that you can walk through the metal detector without setting it off?"

Taylour looked up and saw Philip standing with his phone at his ear about twenty feet away. She scowled and hung up the phone, placed it in the tray next to the metal detector, and then walked through again.

Beep, beep, beep.

Giving a grunt of disgust, she patted herself down and realized that the broach she put on that morning was the culprit. She took it off, put it in the tray with her phone, and walked through a third time.

Beep, beep, beep.

"Ma'am, please step over here." The security guard waved a wand over her, and it pulsated when it passed over her sling.

"Jimmie, you know me. You know that I don't have a weapon."

Jimmie puffed up his chest and said, "Ma'am, would you please remove your sling." Taylour saw that he tried to hide his grin as he said it, and then Taylour remembered him as the third baseman from last night's game.

"Laugh it up, why don't you. Just because we kicked your butts last night."

The Fallen Body

Snickering out loud with his other security guard buddies, he waved her on. "Ms. Dixxon, you were out by a mile."

She grabbed her briefcase in a huff and walked towards the elevator with Philip at her heels. She pushed the up button, read the "Elevator Out of Order" sign, and let out another grunt of frustration. "This is just not my day."

She turned towards the stairs, walked up to the second floor, and headed down the hallway. Philip followed without saying a word. Just as she was about to enter, he reached in front of her and blocked her way to the door. She tried to go around him, but he stepped in front. She looked up at him in annoyance.

In the warmth of the courthouse, Taylour noticed Philip's scar for the first time. It ran a pallid straight line, just below his hairline on his right temple, for about two inches, after which it faded from view. It may have been a long forgotten wound from a stray bullet, or maybe he cracked his head on the edge of a desk as a child. She noticed that he touched it subconsciously while he was staring at her. Maybe it was a reminder of some past indiscretion, but she couldn't take her eyes off of it.

With a grin, he said, "Do I have your attention now?"

"Mr. Davidson, please. I'm late for court."

"Please, call me Philip."

"Sorry, yes, Philip. I need to get inside, or the judge will give me a talking to that I am just not in the mood to receive this morning."

"That's OK, I know the judge."

She squinted at him, turned her head to the side, and then recognition crossed her face. "You mean, Judge Davidson? He's your--?"

The Fallen Body

"Judge Davidson is my father. He will understand that I need to talk with you, even for a moment."

Taylour rubbed the back of her neck and assumed a stiff posture. "Look, I don't know what game you're playing here, but I need to get inside."

"Our client, Sarah Cockrell Baines, whom I am protecting, is, ah, having some troubles adjusting to her current situation."

Taylour squinted at him, her head cocked to the side. "What kind of troubles?"

Philip shifted his feet and looked down. "Well, uh, she needs attention."

"What kind of attention?"

Philip shifted his weight on his feet. "She needs female attention. Someone to talk to. Someone to share things with."

"But we already decided that any contact from me should come through you. Do you want to change that arrangement?"

"No, but I have some thoughts on who I might get to help me."

"Who's with Sarah now?"

"She's at her aunt's house, getting a few more things. Don't worry, I've got someone watching her."

"So who do you want her to talk to?"

"Um, uh, she's someone that I've worked with for many years." Philip suddenly couldn't look Taylour in the eyes, averting his gaze to the side.

She picked up on his discomfort immediately. "Oh, OK." She picked up her briefcase, pushed past him, and marched up to the front of the courtroom.

She sat down next to Mr. Larson without even greeting him. Mr. Larson studied her, opened his mouth as if to say something, but he didn't. He sat back without saying a word.

The bailiff, who had disappeared into the judge's chambers when Taylour had arrived, returned and announced to those in the room, "All rise, the Honorable Judge Kenneth Davidson is presiding."

Chapter 24

"Ms. Dixxon, I couldn't help but wonder if there was something wrong when you came into court this morning." Mr. Larson said.

Taylour had gone through the required actions with the court, and even got a favorable ruling by the judge on her motion to dismiss. However, her mind was clearly elsewhere when she gathered her notes together.

"Sorry. I was a bit distracted by a conversation that I had."

"Is everything OK?"

Taylour averted her gaze and mumbled that everything was fine. After looking at her more closely, he thanked her for her efforts and walked out with his family.

The truth was, she was bothered by what Philip had told her earlier. And it bothered her that Sarah having feelings for Philip upset her so much. Was she having her own fantasies for Philip? Pfft! That wasn't it. Or was it?

She put her notes in her briefcase and headed out the door. As she walked to her car, she glanced at her watch. Realizing that she had a couple of hours before her next appointment, she decided to leave her car parked at the courthouse and have lunch at Ronnie's Chicken.

Taylour ordered the fried chicken, which came with creamed corn, lettuce salad, mashed potatoes, and the best buttermilk biscuits she had ever tasted.

A few minutes later, Taylour noticed Philip enter the restaurant. He went straight to the opposite side of the small dining area and proceeded to scan the menu. She scrunched down a little, so he didn't notice her. After he had finished ordering his food, he turned slightly in the booth and saw her. He pointed at himself and then at her as if asking if he could join her, but she shook her head. However, he gathered up his things anyway and marched to her table.

When he got closer and was just about to sit down, he stopped. "I thought you weren't expecting someone."

"What? No, I mean, I'm *not* expecting someone. Were you thinking that I was expecting someone? That's why I shook my head. No, please, have a seat." She put her hands to her hair as if to straighten it out, and then gave him her best insincere smile.

"So, how did it go with my father?"

"Uh... Oh, yes, your father, the Honorable Davidson. Fine. I got my client's suit dismissed." She grabbed the napkin. "I mean, the suit against my client. Dismissed, that is." She unfolded her napkin, but then dropped her fork on the floor. She put her hand to her forehead in embarrassment.

"Here, let me get you another fork." Philip reached over to the table next to them and grabbed a fresh set of wrapped up silverware. Their hands brushed up against each other as she took the napkin from him.

She blushed, but quickly recovered. "So, Philip, what brings you to town?"

The Fallen Body

"Oh, I had some errands to run." He stared at her as if trying to discern her secret thoughts, but she was not going to give him that satisfaction.

He has to know that I am avoiding the subject. "Like what?"

"Just boring office stuff." He looked away, as if not wanting to divulge too much.

He is playing it cool, though. That's kinda sweet, actually. "Yeah, I know how that is."

Just then, the waitress brought them their food, so they both dug in, not having to talk.

"Mm, this is good!" Philip said between bites.

Does he know that he has gravy on his chin? Taylour instinctively reached up with her finger and motioned to him to wipe his chin. "Yeah, I eat here all the time."

"I can see why. It's delicious."

They made more small talk until they both finished their food. As they conversed, she learned that, in addition to his father being a District Court judge, he had a brother who was a highway patrolman. His brother, who was younger than Philip, lived within twenty minutes of Marlinsville and had two young kids, a boy and a girl. His mother had recently passed away from breast cancer. Taylour felt a twinge of nostalgia as she recalled her own mother's bout with lung cancer. Over their conversation, the tension that Taylour felt towards Philip dissipated.

During a lull, she happened to glance at her watch. "Oh! I didn't realize how late it had gotten. I've got an appointment in 10 minutes at my office. Gotta go."

She strode to the front and paid her bill, and was just about to walk out when she realized that she had left her briefcase in the booth, so she turned around abruptly and almost ran Philip over, who was right behind her.

The Fallen Body

"Uh, sorry. Forgot my--" Philip handed her briefcase over and smirked slightly.

"Needing this, I assume?" His relaxed demeanor was no longer as disconcerting as it was before. What was disconcerting was how she felt like a bumbling idiot whenever he looked at her.

"Thanks." She took her briefcase and slung it over her shoulder. Thinking that he was not going to follow her to her car, she said good-bye and turned to walk back towards the courthouse.

He stood there, undecided, and then he hastened to catch up with her. As he fell in beside her, she flinched and slowed down.

"Sorry. I didn't know you were parked over here." Taylour glanced again at her watch, mumbled under her breath, and picked up her pace again.

Philip kept up, and once they reached her car, he opened the door for her.

Before closing it, he put his hand on the top of the car and said, "I enjoyed our lunch."

She thanked him for joining her and waved as she drove away. As Taylour drove the short distance to her office, she found herself replaying their conversation over and over again.

She blushed when she realized that she couldn't wait to see him again.

Chapter 25

Taylour looked at the time and saw that it was nearly 7 p.m. Taylour leaned back in her chair and closed her eyes as if to shut out the world. The stress of running an office and practicing law at the same time was sometimes too much. But what else was she going to do?

Betty was long gone, so she decided to head home. The temperature had dropped several degrees as soon as the sun went down, so she hastened to her car and got in. As she pulled up to her house, she saw a familiar figure rocking on her porch.

"Spencer? What in the world are you doing here?"

"Hey, Auntie Taylour! How's it hangin'?"

Spencer Dixxon, 23 year old son of her older brother Victor, was standing on her porch. Behind him, Taylour saw a US Army duffle bag with some of its contents spilled out, leaving a trail back to the rocking chair.

She motioned him to come over with her index finger. He shuffled down the steps with a sly grin on his face and silently stood before her. She looked him over briefly -- *why is he wearing a black Aerosmith concert shirt?* − and then reached up to hug him awkwardly with her good arm.

"It's good to see you, Spencer, but what are you doing here? Does your dad know that you're here?"

"My *father* could care less if I was here or in Timbuktu."

Squinting her eyes at him, Taylour said, "Well, I happen to think that he *does* care where you are, and you are gonna tell him just as soon as you get your stuff inside."

Breaking out into a huge grin, Spencer quickly tossed his stuff into the bag and dragged it with him. He dropped it by the stairs and quickly headed towards the kitchen.

"Hold it, mister. Not before you call your father." Taylour stood with her phone extended towards him.

He reluctantly took it from her, but instead of dialing the number, he said, "He's not even home, and I don't know where he is."

Taylour took the phone back and dialed a number. "Let's find out where he is, shall we?" She let it ring until his voicemail came on. "Hey, Victor, it's your sister. Guess who showed up on my doorstep unannounced? Yep, it's your son. He's fine and he's safe, but I need you to call me as soon as you get this. You know the number. Bye."

Pointing the phone at him, she said, "Tell me what's going on."

Spencer tossed his hands up in the air and walked into the kitchen. He pulled the bread out of the pantry, dug around in her fridge, and made himself a ham and cheese sandwich. He glanced up at her. "Did you want me to make you one?"

"No, I want you to tell me why you are here."

The Fallen Body

"He is ruining my life! I can't stand the 'Do this' or 'Do that' or 'Why don't you have a job?' Doesn't he get that I'm just chillin', waiting for my thing to come along?"

He slapped the meat on the bread, "He doesn't care about what *I* want. What *my* dreams are." He waved his hands at Taylour. "Yes, I have dreams, big dreams!"

Standing awkwardly with her right arm folded around her immovable left arm, she asked, "What are those dreams exactly, Spencer? Huh? Tell me one dream that you have."

"You know. Dreams. I dunno exactly, but I'll know it when I see it."

"So you decided to cross the state in search of what, exactly?"

"An opportunity, Aunt Taylour! An opportunity! That's what I am searching for."

Putting the phone down, she took a huge breath and let it out. "OK, I'll let you stay..." He raised his arms in victory. "for a week." He dropped his hands, but then perked up.

"Thanks, Aunt Taylour, you won't regret this."

Taylour gave him a half-hearted smile, but on the inside, she asked herself what she was getting herself into. *I hope I don't regret this.*

Chapter 26

Taylour slept fitfully that night, tossing and turning in her bed, her dreams dark and foreboding. As she woke up before dawn, she felt anxious about the near future and what it could possibly bring. It bothered her enough that she decided she needed to let off some steam, so she got dressed in her jogging attire, grabbed her iPod Shuffle and ear buds, and slipped out of her house just as the sun peeped over the horizon.

It was a chilly morning, upper 40s, but there were no clouds in the sky, so the sun was expected to warm the flat prairie land today. She quickly stretched her muscles, and then started with a brisk walk. Concerned that her left arm might give her problems, she started with a slow jog. It felt good, not too much discomfort. As she picked up the pace, running passed the barbed wire fences and the golden fields, she could smell newly turned earth, which had a way of cleansing her mind. She enjoyed being outside, listening to her New Age music, and felt the tension dissipate as she ran along the side of the road.

After about two miles, she decided to head back, but took a different route than normal. She headed south along U.S. Highway 377, which ran parallel to the train

The Fallen Body

tracks that bisected Marlinsville. As she got to the intersection, she headed west towards her ranch house that laid a few miles down the road. The air was already starting to get warmer, and the sweat came out more profusely, cleansing her body of toxins. She grunted in satisfaction, slowed down to a hard walk, took several deep breaths through her nose, and then felt much better than before. That feeling didn't last long.

As she walked through her front door, her landline phone started ringing. The caller ID said "Dixxon, Victor" so she pushed the green Talk button.

"It's about time you called me back, big brother."

Silence on the other line, and then a woman's voice spoke. "Hi, Taylour, it's me, Linda."

"Oh, uh. Sorry, Linda, I was expecting your husband to call. Is he there?"

A slight hesitation, and then Linda responded, "Victor is not here right now, but I wanted to return your message. I'm glad that Spencer is OK."

Linda was Spencer's stepmother and had married Victor last summer after his divorce several years ago. She had never been married before and was several years younger than Victor. Taylour had met her only a couple of times, first at their wedding, and then when Taylour visited them for Thanksgiving last year. She remembered that Linda had seemed a bit overwhelmed with everything, the meal preparations, the traditional football game with the neighbors, an early 20s stepson and his quirkiness.

"Thank you for calling me back, Linda. It was quite a shock to see him on my doorstep yesterday without warning."

The Fallen Body

A longer pause this time. "Well, I appreciate you taking him in. It's been so hard these last few months, with my pregnancy and all, you--"

"Wait, did you say that you are pregnant? Congratulations! That's just like my brother to not tell me something important like that. When are you due?"

"Not until March, so there is still a lot to get ready for, and we're going to paint the guest room and get a crib and all the other stuff that a person needs." Taylour heard a sigh, but stayed silent. "Spencer's been, well, a handful, to say it nicely."

Taylour put her hand to her head as she felt a headache coming on. "Linda, I appreciate your situation. I admire you for marrying my brother and the circumstances that you married into. You have a lot of courage to do that."

"Well, I love Victor. More than I thought I would. It's been hard adjusting to being a wife to Victor and a mom to Spencer." Taylour heard a crack in Linda's voice. "Maria has been nonexistent, not even sure where she is." Maria was Spencer's biological mother. "I-I'm at my wit's end!"

"Linda, I understand. Will you have Victor call me ASAP? I'll talk it over with him and maybe we can come to some kind of a *short-term* arrangement, OK?"

Sniffling, Linda said, "That would be great, Taylour! We would be so grateful to you, honestly."

Taylour hung up the phone, shook her head, and headed upstairs because she had an idea. Even though it was a weekday, she had several chores that needed to get done, but with her injury, she wasn't going to be able to do half of them. The solution was snoring softly in her guest room.

The Fallen Body

She pounded on the door to announce her entrance, and then walked in to find Spencer sprawled across the bed, the bed covers in disarray and not covering enough of her nephew, who apparently slept in tighty whities and nothing else. She grimaced, averted her gaze, and shook him with her one good hand. "Get up! If you're going to stay here, then you need to earn your keep."

A soft groan was all she got for her efforts, so she shook him again, harder. "Spencer, it is time to get up and about. C'mon. I have a lot of work for you to do." A louder groan this time as Spencer wiped the sleepiness from his eyes.

"What time is it?"

"It's time to get some work done. Look, if you want to stay here, I cannot have you sleeping away the day. There's a fence that needs painting, some last minute weeds that need pulling, and I've got a gimpy arm." She plugged her nose as she turned to go. "If you want any breakfast, you'd better be down in five minutes sharp."

"Ugh."

"Did you just say 'Ugh' in my house? We don't say 'Ugh,' we say 'Yes ma'am!' and 'No ma'am!' and 'How high would you prefer I jump, ma'am!'"

"Ugh, er, I mean, yes ma'am."

"Good, that's a start. Now, get ready to enjoy the fruits of hard labor."

Instead of showering, she headed back downstairs to the kitchen to scramble some eggs and fry up some sausage patties. As she worked, she made a mental list of all the things that needed to get done.

By the time Spencer showed up for breakfast, she was cheerfully humming to the tune of "Whistle While You Work." She laid out the food on the counter and said, "Good morning, sleepy head. Hungry?"

The Fallen Body

"Famished." He grabbed a fork and took three of the four sausage patties, a huge scoop of eggs, and filled up a tall glass of orange juice. He moved over to the table, where he shoveled his food in. He was halfway done by the time Taylour sat down with her plate.

"So, Auntie Taylour, what is on the agenda for today?" Spencer asked with his mouth full of food.

"Don't talk with your mouth full, and call me Taylour, OK? You're an adult now, and I'm way too young to be someone's 'Auntie.' We've got a fence to paint on the south side of the yard, the spray paint and brushes are already in the barn. While you're doing that, I need to run by my office to work."

"You mean that I have to do that all by myself? Can I come too?"

"No, you need to stay here while I work alone. I've only got a few things that I need to get done, but I need some peace and quiet to do it in. Since you've got two good hands, you get to be my little minion, so to speak."

Casting his eyes downward, he said, "OK. But later, I want to see your office. I've done some filing jobs before, so I can totally organize your workspace."

"Sure! Let me just fire the secretary that I've had for the past 10 years and start fresh. Maybe that'll be your big opportunity!"

"You don't have to be sarcastic or anything. I'm just asking."

"I've got everything under control at the office. Right now, I just need someone to help me get things straight here."

"Am I gonna get paid, or somethin'? I might be more motivated if it meant that I'd be getting remuneration for my efforts."

"Remuneration? What 23 year old says that?"

The Fallen Body

"I read things, OK? I have to be properly motivated to do work."

"How about I send you back to your dad? I happened to talk to Linda this morning. When were you going to tell me that she was pregnant?"

"Uh, don't get me started on that. I love Linda, but when she is hormonal, watch out!"

"Hormonal? It's a wonder that you haven't found that 'someone special' with the progressive thinking spewing forth from that Neanderthal brain of yours."

"Neanderthal? Who you calling a Neanderthal?"

"You! I'm calling you a Neanderthal!" Taylour took a deep breath and pointed her finger at Spencer. "Listen, I don't want to fight with you right now. I will pay you what I think you're worth, but this kind of talk is decreasing your worth to me, not increasing it, so watch it, OK?"

Spencer backed off. "OK. Sorry."

"I accept your apology. Now, go get some work clothes on while I do the dishes and I'll get you started. After that, I'm gonna run through the shower real quick, which will give you a good head start on me. If you're done by the time I get back from the office, I'll give you something else to do."

They got up from the table and Spencer went upstairs to change his clothes. Taylour did the dishes, and then they walked out together to the barn. She showed him where the supplies were and where she wanted him to paint, and then went inside. She showered quickly, and then dried her strawberry blonde hair. *Do I see some gray hair poking through?*

Just then, the phone rang. "Hello?"

"Taylour, how are you?"

The Fallen Body

"I've been better, Vincent. I suppose you've talked with Linda about what is going on?"

"Yes, and I can't thank you enough. Things have been crazy around here. You taking him in is going to be a big help."

"Wait, taking him in? What did Linda tell you exactly?"

A burst of air being expelled came through the phone. "That you were, ah, gonna take care of Spencer."

"Vincent! That is not what I said. I told Linda that I would watch him for the short-term. I am certainly not prepared to take him on full-time!"

"Look, Taylour, right now I need your help, OK? Linda has been under a lot of pressure, and the last thing she needs is to get all worked up over Spencer. The doc said she needs her rest, and Spencer is just not helping out around here."

"Vincent, I've got too much to take care of around here. I've got to help solve a murder, for which I feel totally inadequate. I can't handle some snot-nosed, overgrown teenager in my life right now!"

She heard the floorboards creak in the hallway and jerked her head around just in time to see Spencer disappear around the corner. She cringed when she heard the slam of the guest room door.

"Look, Vincent, I gotta go. We'll talk more about this later." She hung up.

She finished getting dressed in some sweats and a loose fitting sweater, and then went to Spencer's room. She knocked softly on the door, but there was no answer. "Spencer? Are you OK?" Nothing. She went to open the door, but thought better about that and said to the closed door, "I'll be back in a few hours. We'll talk then, OK?" Silence.

The Fallen Body

She grabbed her keys, glanced one more time at the closed bedroom door, and then left.

Chapter 27

Taylour drove quickly to her office and went inside. She retrieved the files that she needed from the cabinet and sat down at her desk. As she worked, her thoughts would occasionally wander to Spencer, but she quickly brought her mind back to the tasks at hand. Before she knew it, she was all caught up. She glanced at the clock on her desk, which read 12:45 p.m., put her things away, and decided to pick up some burritos for two to go from Tortilla Casa.

She knew the owner, Franco Acosta, as she had defended him on a wrongful termination suit that could have gotten ugly quick. Taylour stepped in and found that the plaintiff had an extensive history of suing her previous employers. She had saved Tortilla Casa from financial ruin, and Franco was eternally grateful to her for her efforts. He insisted on giving her the employee discount whenever she came in.

Franco greeted her warmly when she walked in and sat down. She took in the aroma of salsa and homemade tortillas as he personally took her order. The burritos were made with either beef or chicken, with refried beans, salsa, grated American cheese, onions and rice, and one was enough to feed two people. She ordered three, thanked Franco for his generosity, and drove home.

When she pulled in, she noticed that the fence was not painted. Furious at herself because of her careless words earlier, she took the food inside and yelled for Spencer to come down and eat. She sat down and ate half of her burrito. When Spencer didn't come down, she put the food away in the fridge and trudged up the stairs.

"Spencer? Are you there?" No answer. She slowly opened up the door to his room, but it was empty. He had made the bed, and his bag had been placed neatly on the floor. Taylour furrowed her brow and wandered outside to the barn.

When she poked her head inside, she saw no one. "Spencer, are you in here?" Still nothing. She started to get worried. *Where did he wander off to?*

Taylour turned around at the sound of a car pulling up. It was a squad car, with Marlinsville Police scrawled across the side panel. Taylour recognized the officer that stepped out of the car.

"Officer Daniels? What are you doing here?"

"Hey, Ms. Dixxon, I found someone who says that he belongs to you."

He walked around the passenger side and opened the door. Spencer slunk out of the car, his hands handcuffed in front of him. Officer Daniels retrieved his key, unlocked the cuffs, and gently guided him to Taylour.

"Found him with some black spray paint just about to make graffiti on the overpass. While the others that were with him scattered as I pulled up, he stayed behind." Taylour's mouth fell as her eyes widened. She started blinking rapidly, and stuttered out her thanks for bringing him back.

The Fallen Body

"We won't press charges if he promises not to do it again. I know who some of his buddies were, not the best crowd to be hanging out with around here. Bunch of troublemakers is what they are."

Taylour brought her shaking right hand to her forehead and shook her head repeatedly. "Officer Daniels, I give you my word." She stared laser beams at Spencer, who was kicking the dirt with his feet and avoiding eye contact. "This will *not* happen again."

As the police car drove away, she grabbed Spencer by the arm and led him inside. After slamming the front door closed, she started pacing back and forth. Spencer just stood there, motionless, and waited for the storm to come. Every few minutes she would let out a guttural sound and punctuate her frustration by throwing her right hand up into the air. Bemused, Spencer shifted his weight, which finally got a reaction from Taylour.

"Wipe that grin off your face, mister. I have half a mind to send you back to your father on the next bus out of town! I am this close to pressing charges *myself* if I have to deal any more with such nonsense. Y' hear me?"

Spencer went to open his mouth, but she cut him off with her index finger. "I did not *ask* you to come here. I do not *need* this aggravation." Spencer squirmed, but said nothing. "But you are family, and family sticks together."

"Does that mean that I can stay?"

She stood right up into his face "If I so much as *hear* that you are hanging out with those lowlifes, it is 'Ciao, baby.' *Capisce?*"

He lowered his head to one side and squinted his eyes. "Huh?"

"Look it up!" she yelled as she stormed off.

Chapter 28

Roman listened to the latest recordings made from his bugs in Taylour's office, but there was no discussion about the murder. In addition, there had been no mention of where Sarah was. A loud exhale escaped from Roman, and then he slowly lifted himself up. It was time to turn up the heat.

He pulled out his phone and dialed.

"Law Offices of Taylour Dixxon, this is Betty. How may I help you?"

"Ah, yes, I was told to call this number as I am trying to reach my sister, Sarah Cockrell."

A slight pause, and then, "May I ask who's calling?"

"This is her brother, Blaine Cockrell."

Another pause, this time a bit longer. "Mr. Cockrell, I am unable to provide that to you over the phone. Would it be possible for you to come by our office?"

Roman hung up without answering. Cursing out loud, he took some deep breaths to calm himself down. After a few minutes of breathing in through his nose and out through his mouth, he felt more in control.

The direct approach was not going to work, and he did not want to expose himself and blow his cover. While he might have to resort to force to get what he wanted at some point in the future, he preferred to squeeze slowly, like an unseen force around his prey, so that he could minimize his risk of being discovered.

If he was going to get what he wanted, he would have to try something else.

* * *

"Well, that was interesting." Betty said out loud.

"What was that, Betty?" Taylour shouted from the break room.

"I just got a call from someone who claimed to be Sarah's brother."

Taylour popped her head out. "Sarah doesn't have a brother."

"I know."

"What did he sound like?"

Betty thought for a moment. "There was something about his voice, almost like he had an accent." She shrugged her shoulders. "The conversation was too short for me to know for sure."

Chapter 29

Roman decided that he needed to apply some pressure as a means of intimidating her. He brainstormed some ideas, discarding them one by one as either being too brazen or too unpractical, until he came across a real possibility. He spent some time in his motel room doing some research on his laptop. There was one critical piece missing, and it took him awhile to find it, but when he did, he knew that his plan would work. It had to. He tried poking holes in his strategy and found a few vulnerabilities, but he knew that he could plug those holes in with plausible excuses.

He was going to exploit the relationship between Betty and Taylour. While they appeared to be close, Betty actually had a secret that, if exposed, could force her to give up where Sarah was hiding. Betty Graham had a gambling problem.

It had started out innocently enough on an Internet website. Betty thought she had a foolproof system for winning at blackjack. She even won a few hundred dollars at first, but steadily lost after that. She started borrowing against the equity in her house, but she never seemed to get a good winning streak going. According to his sources, she was in hock to the tune of nearly $18,000.

Roman was confident that if he approached it right with Betty, it would pay off tenfold, and she would be none the wiser.

* * *

Roman got up early Wednesday morning and drove to Betty's eggshell clapboard home. Her car was still in the driveway, so he got out of his car, walked up to the driver's side, and placed a sealed envelope on her windshield wiper. He glanced around to make sure that he had not been seen, and when satisfied, he scurried back to the Yukon. He took up his post across the street and down a few houses. He didn't have to wait long as Betty came out promptly at ten minutes to 7 o'clock.

Roman put his binoculars up to his eyes and focused the lens on her. He saw her open the envelope and read its contents, and then smiled when she placed her hand on her car to steady herself. She pulled her car door open, jumped into the front seat, and sped off. Roman drove to the intersection and turned right. He positioned himself at the far end of the McDonald's parking lot and waited.

At 6:58 a.m. the disposable phone that he purchased yesterday rang, and he picked it up after the fifth ring.

"Do exactly what I say. Meet me in 10 minutes at the McDonald's parking lot. Go to the black GMC Yukon and get into the passenger seat."

"H-How do I know you won't hurt me?"

"You will just have to trust me." He hung up the phone and waited.

At exactly 7:09 a.m. he saw Betty pull up next to his Yukon and got out. Her gaze darted around before she opened his door and got in. Roman stared straight ahead and said nothing.

The Fallen Body

"W-Who are you?"

"You work for Taylour Dixxon, correct?"

Betty shifted in her seat. "Yes. How did you know that?"

Roman kept his eyes forward. He tossed a thick envelope over to her. "There is five grand in there now, no questions asked. If you give me the information that I am seeking to my satisfaction, you will get another thirteen grand."

"You haven't answered my questions. Who are you and how do you know that I work for Taylour Dixxon?"

"I need to know where Sarah Baines is located."

"Or else?"

Roman turned his eyes to Betty and gave her a hard, cold stare. He leaned in close, got right up into her face, and whispered, "Or else Taylour dies." He slowly pulled out his .22 Colt and pressed it up against Betty's side. "It would not be quick and painless. It would be right here, through the left kidney and out the stomach. She would bleed, and it would be a slow and excruciating death." He poked her with the muzzle, which made her flinch.

"I-I don't know where Sarah is at, b-but I could find out."

He pulled the gun away. "Who knows, if you play your cards right, she might not suspect a thing, and you could keep your job. You are, after all, indispensable."

Betty's body odor filled the car as her lips trembled. With her hand shaking, she held the envelope to her chest and left the Yukon. Roman watched as she fumbled with her keys, dropping them on the hard pavement. He gave a bemused look as she finally managed to get into her car and bolt from the parking lot as if from a slingshot. *That was easier than I thought.*

Chapter 30

Betty rushed through the door of the office, her eyes puffy and red, and dropped her purse onto her chair. She rolled into the tiny bathroom and closed the door. As she gripped the sink, she stared at herself in the mirror. *What have I done?*

She splashed water on her face to cool herself down and thought that maybe she should just go home. Coming to the office meant having to answer questions and she needed time to think, to come up with a plan. She set her jaw, pushed her shoulders back, and fled out the bathroom door.

"Whoa! Slow down, there," said Taylour as she rounded the corner at the same time. Betty pulled up, startled, and apologized for almost knocking Taylour down.

Seeing Betty's quivering chin, Taylour asked, "Is everything OK, Betty?"

Averting her gaze, Betty said, "I'm alright."

"You don't look alright. Is something bothering you? How is your mother doing?"

"Ah, she's... ah. She's fine. I mean, she's not doing well. S-She's had a turn for the worse. Bad heart. She asked me to, ah... to come and visit her because she's not doing too well. So I, ah, need to go to see her. I know that this is sudden, and I understand if you can't let me go, but I do have vacation days that I haven't used, even though I know that I should be giving you more notice than this, but I just talked to her this morning and she, ah, isn't, er, she wants me to come now, so I'd better go now."

"Of course, Betty, of course. You need to take care of your mom." Taylour cocked her head to one side and narrowed her eyes, but said nothing more.

Betty cleared her throat and turned away. She quickly grabbed her purse and hurried out.

Taylour went back to her office and slumped down in her chair. *That was strange!* She exhaled and slowly twirled her chair around, deep in thought. Finally, she pushed herself up out of her chair and walked to Betty's desk. The phone rang, so she answered it. It was a telemarketer asking for the owner of the business, and when Taylour said that she was the owner, the voice on the other end asked if she was interested in -- click. Taylour hung up the phone, but barely had enough time before another call came through, and then another right after that. She threw her hands up in the air and was about to hide in her office when she saw a piece of paper that seemed out of place. She picked it up.

It was a photocopy of an Internet gambling account. Betty's account, by the name at the top of the paper, with a red marker circling a number, -$17,895. There was a phone number scrawled at the bottom of the statement, with a simple message in big, black letters:

GIVE ME WHAT I WANT, AND I CAN MAKE THIS ALL GO AWAY

The Fallen Body

Taylour's hand flew to her mouth as she stifled a gasp. The paper floated noiselessly to the ground.

Chapter 31

There were days when she really did not like being cooped up in a tiny room, with little space to maneuver around the boxes and stacks of files. Where clients didn't demand so much of your time and attention, and then give so little in return. Where you constantly feel under-appreciated and under-rewarded. Today was one of those days.

Taylour did her best to answer the phone and do her other work, but by lunch time she was exhausted and decided to call it quits. She looked one more time at the statement, dialed the number for the tenth time, and for the tenth time she got a fast busy signal. She made a note to herself to contact someone she knew on the police force who owed her a favor so that she could do a trace on any phone records that might exist, but she didn't have much hope that the trace would lead anywhere. She also tried Betty's cell phone again, but the call went straight to voice mail. She didn't leave a message.

It bothered her that Betty wasn't picking up, but she recognized her behavior earlier as classic guilt symptoms. The stuttering, the lying, the quivering chin, the fast talking. She had seen it many times in clients that she knew were guilty. *Why didn't I see the signs before she left? I might have been able to help.* She vowed to swing by Betty's house on the way back home.

She turned the answering machine on and gathered her things. As she got in her car, she shook her head and wondered if anything else would go wrong.

Taylour slowed as she neared Betty's house. She noticed that Betty's car was gone, but she stopped anyway and knocked on the front door. No answer. She tried opening the door, but it was locked.

She tried to peer in the window, but the blinds were down and blocked her view, so she tiptoed around to the back and tried the sliding door. Locked as well. She couldn't see past the opaque curtain, so she went to the side to see if any of the windows were open, but they were sealed shut.

With an impatient snort and muttering under her breath, she made her way back to her car and drove off.

As she pulled into her property, she saw a border collie puppy digging up her flower bed by her stairs. She rushed out and grabbed the offending animal. "No, no! Bad dog!" She looked at the collar and saw the name "Dog." *Very original.*

Just then, Spencer came out and said, "There you are, I've been looking all over for you." Taking the dog from Taylour, he nuzzled his nose into Dog's fur and made cooing noises.

"What is the meaning of... this?" Taylour asked, pointing at the puppy.

"This is Dog. Dog, meet your Auntie Taylour. Taylour, meet Dog. You're so cute. Yes you are!"

"Spencer! We don't need a dog."

The Fallen Body

Covering the ears of Dog, Spencer shushed her. "We do need a dog. A dog to keep us safe. A dog to keep us company. Yes we do." More nuzzling.

Taylour rolled her eyes and pushed past them. "He's your dog and your responsibility, not mine. I've got plenty of problems of my own. I've got to find a new temporary secretary, and I don't need this."

Spencer perked up his head. "You need a new secretary? I could do it."

Taylour stopped and looked at him with squinty eyes. "You? Ah, no. I need someone who knows what they're doing."

"I know what to do, Auntie Taylour!"

"Call me Taylour!"

"Taylour, I know that I didn't get off to a great start here, but really, I can help. I know how to answer the phone, I am organized. You just need to show me the layout and I'll have it humming along in no time."

"But I need someone who has experience. I don't make enough to hire you and someone else."

"But I'll work for free, at least for the first week or so. I can be your office manager."

Taylour ran the numbers in her head, and shrugged her shoulders. "I could certainly use the help, and there certainly is no shortage of work. I'm in a bind."

Spencer placed the puppy on the porch next to his new food bowl and gave Taylour a bright-eyed look.

"OK, you can work for me, on one condition. We need to get you some office attire, so we are going shopping."

Spencer grasped her by the shoulders and twirled around with her. "Taylour Dixxon, you are not going to regret this. Finally, my opportunity!"

Chapter 32

Sarah slept fitfully that evening. She had the same nightmare as a few days ago, but this time she saw the enemy advancing, the hatred in their eyes and the frothing of the horses as they clamored towards her. She felt real fear, as if she was in mortal danger, and woke up from her legs thrashing.

At breakfast, Sarah asked, "What's on the schedule for today?"

Philip mulled that over before answering. "Well, I've got some errands to run. I've got someone that will stay with you while I'm gone, someone that I trust."

"Oh? Who is it?"

"Her name's Karen, and she's been a Texas Ranger for almost twenty years. I trust her with my life." He glanced at his watch. "She should be here any minute."

He got up from the table and excused himself. Sarah finished her breakfast and cleaned up.

Outside, an identical silver Ford Explorer pulled up next to Philip's vehicle and a woman hopped out. A hard knock on the door, and then Sarah opened it.

"Hi, you must be Sarah. I'm Karen Russell." She thrust her hand out, and Sarah shook it lightly. The handshake from Karen crushed her fingers, and then Karen swept past her.

She was dressed in jeans and boots, with a flannel shirt and a denim jacket. Sarah looked her over and saw a fortyish woman, a little taller than herself and a bit on the plump side, with her black and grayish hair pulled back into a ponytail. She stood with her hands on her hips and turned to Sarah.

"Philip gettin' dressed?"

Sarah nodded her head. "Yes, we just had breakfast together."

"Karen! How are you!" Philip rushed into the room and gave Karen a hug. "It's been a long time."

Karen blushed. "Yes, it has, y' big lug." She lightly tapped him on the shoulder with her fist.

Sarah's face looked sullen, but she said nothing.

"It looks like you've met Sarah. Look, I appreciate you doing this on such short notice. I need to run some errands, which will take most of the day."

"When will you be back?" Sarah asked.

"Oh, not sure, exactly. Probably late." Philip grabbed his jacket and headed for the door. Sarah followed him out and stood on the porch as he pulled out. She waved goodbye and continued to linger until his Explorer faded from view in a cloud of dust.

Sarah's hands began to tremble, so she folded them across her chest and went back inside.

Because Sarah wanted to avoid talking with Karen, she announced that she was going to take a shower. Karen nodded her assent, and then made herself comfortable on the sofa.

After a long, hot shower, Sarah emerged from the back with a novel and sat on the opposite end of the room in the recliner. She swiveled her back to Karen, hoping to discourage any conversation.

"So, Sarah, tell me a little bit about y'self."

Sarah sighed, and then slowly turned her chair. "There's not much to tell, really."

An awkward pause. "Well, then, let me tell y' a little about me. I'm divorced, got twin girls who just started college this fall at Texas A&M, and--"

"I'm sorry, Karen, I don't mean to be rude, but I have a headache and I really don't feel like talking."

Karen lifted both her hands as if in surrender. "Fine by me. But let me tell you one thing, and one thing only." She leaned towards Sarah. "You don't want to start somethin' with Philip. He's all business and you'll only get your heart burned, if y' know what I mean."

Sarah's eyes gaped open. "How did you know?"

"Honey, I know that look that you gave him, as well as the look that you gave me. That fire you shot towards me would've melted steel."

Sarah couldn't help but smile. "Was it that obvious?"

"It was to me, but you know men. They don't get things like that, or they choose to ignore them. My guess is that Philip doesn't want to hurt your feelings by bringing it up."

"I-I'm afraid to talk with him about it. I don't want to ruin the friendship that we have developed."

"My advice is, don't bring it up. Keep your feelings to yourself, but realize that he won't compromise his assignment by letting his feelings get in the way." Karen sat back and averted her eyes. "I know from personal experience."

Sarah's jaw dropped. "You?"

"Yep." She stared back at Sarah with softness. "I was vulnerable, just like you are, and we were working a case together. I had just signed divorce papers, so I was already an emotional wreck, and I made the mistake of telling him how I felt about him." Karen smirked. "I'll never forget the look on his face. You'd a thought that I had run over the family dog."

"What did you do then?"

"I tried to tell him that I was just kidding, that it was all just a joke. Not sure if he believed me, but it was the only thing I could do to lessen the pain and embarrassment." Karen shifted in her seat. "I never brought it up again, and eventually we developed a strong, lasting friendship. I trust him, and he trusts me."

"Thank you. I guess I owe you an apology for the way I acted."

"Nah, don't worry about it. I've got thick skin." Karen slapped her hands on her knees and stood up. "Well, I'm gonna take a look 'round, if you don't mind. Can't be too careful."

Karen opened up the front door, letting in a rush of cool air, and then pulled the door shut. Sarah shivered, and then closed her eyes, pushing the tears back. Her emotions were swirling around and around, and all she wanted at that moment was peace.

But peace would not find her.

Chapter 33

Philip called one of his FBI contacts in the Organized Crime division in the New York office.

"Borelli."

"Philip Davidson here from the Texas Rangers. Look, I'm trying to track down some information about a Dmitri Polzin."

Philip heard some shuffling of papers. "He's a minor player in one of the Russian mob groups, also known as *Bratva*, which means 'brotherhood.' What are you looking for exactly?"

"I am looking for known associates, people that he does business with, as well as any ongoing investigations, if you have any."

"Well, we always keep an eye on certain persons of interest, some of the bigger players. They're not like the Costa Nostra with their familial structure. They are more a loose collective of various organized crime syndicates. They tend to work across borders, if you know what I mean."

"Where do they tend to operate?"

"The largest group is called the Odessa Mafia, and they are concentrated mostly around Brighton Beach,

The Fallen Body

New York, which is the part of Brooklyn that is right along the seacoast. This crime group is believed to be involved in extortion, money laundering, fraud, loan sharking, that kind of thing. They have a fairly recent beginning in the U.S. in the late 1970's and earlier 1980's, and some real bad actors that have been thrown in jail. Some of those are lifers, but a number of them are starting to get released and are going back to their old ways. It's a fascinating history, I tell ya."

"And where does Dmitri Polzin fit into this?"

"Well, it's hard to say exactly, since they are such a hard group to infiltrate, mostly due to language barriers, etc., but Dmitri is known as a brigadier, who works for the *pakhan*, or boss. His main responsibilities are running the criminal operations. The support and security groups act as the buffer between the elite and the working groups so that no one person can bring down the entire group. Rumor has it that Dmitri was somehow involved in the assassination of Sergey Timofeev in 1994. He's one bad dude."

"I appreciate the history lesson. Can I ask you to send me a copy of what he's been involved in recently? I've got a murder investigation going here in Dallas and his name keeps popping up."

"Sure thing, I'll have one of my agents pull together something for you. We've been trying to nail this guy for a long time, but we can never seem to get anything to stick. Maybe you'll get lucky on your end. Take care."

Philip hung up the phone and paused before dialing his next number.

"Hello, can I please speak with Taylour Dixxon?"

"Ah, yeah. Can I ask who's calling?"

"This is Philip Davidson, from the Texas Rangers. Ms. Dixxon knows who I am."

The Fallen Body

The call was put through, and Taylour picked it up on the third ring. "This is Taylour."

"This is Philip. Look, I owe you an apology for how I pushed your buttons the other day, so I was hoping that I could make it up to you by taking you out to dinner tonight. My treat."

"Philip, I am flattered that you want to take me to dinner on such short notice, but are we mixing business with pleasure?"

She was determined not to make this easy for him. Well, two can play that game.

"Wait, are you thinking that I am asking you out on a date?"

"Well, aren't you?" Taylour said. He could hear her chuckle through the phone.

"This is strictly professional." Philip blushed, but caught himself. "I need to apprise you on what is going with the investigation. You know, Neal Baines?"

"I know who you mean. I have time this evening for a 'work meeting' if you are paying."

"Perfect! I will meet you at the Prairie House at 7 p.m."

"Be sure to call ahead for a reservation as they tend to be busy."

"I will do that, thanks for the tip. See you then."

Chapter 34

Taylour hung up the phone quickly and sat back in her chair, her fingers making a fist and curled over her mouth. She did have several questions for him as she still hadn't heard back from her private investigator. She picked up the phone and called, but all she got was his answering machine. Since she had already left three previous messages, she didn't leave another message. However, she was getting irritated at the lack of response. She quickly shot off an email to him, practically pleading with him to call her, or text her, something.

Spencer poked his head in and asked, "Who is Philip Davidson? Someone special?"

"No, he's just someone that..." Taylour paused, trying to define their relationship in her mind, but coming up blank. "Never mind. He and I are going to have a working dinner tonight, so you and Dog are on your own for dinner tonight. There's plenty of leftovers in the fridge, so warm something up."

"Aw, why can't I come? I am your office manager now, and we need to celebrate our new working relationship."

The Fallen Body

"Uh, no. Philip and I have a lot to go over and we don't need to be distracted by you. You and I will go out another time to, uh, celebrate."

Spencer wiggled his eyebrows and said, "I get it. You don't have to tell me twice." Taylour's ears went red as he left, chuckling.

She managed to get a few more hours of solid work done before she decided to leave. She could hear Spencer wrapping up a phone call, so she gathered her papers together that she wanted to go over with Philip and put them in her bag. She turned the light off in her office and ventured out to the reception area.

She was taken aback at how clean the place looked. Spencer had been busy while she had been working. Where Betty had not always been the neatest secretary, with various files stacked up in different piles around her, now the entire desk consisted of the phone, a notepad for taking messages, and the flat screen from his computer. It was wiped clean and there was even a small bouquet of flowers on the edge.

"Spencer, I am impressed! I didn't realize that the desk was so large. It seemed to always be covered in files."

"Oh, well, like I said before, I know how to organize. I have a new filing system that makes it very easy to find what cases are closed, which ones are open, etc. I'll show it to you sometime when you're not in such a hurry. Have fun on your 'date-that-is-not-a-date' with Mr. Davidson."

Taylour left and drove home. On the way, she started to worry that the house was a mess downstairs, but why should that matter, since she certainly was not going to invite Philip home. She blushed again, and put that out of her mind.

The Fallen Body

Once she made it home, she saw Dog again, but this time he loped up to her, wagging his tail like crazy. She noticed dirt in his paws and all up and down his front legs and belly. "Have you been digging again?" She picked him up, looked around furtively, and then nuzzled him. "Don't think that this is going to get you off, mister. You need to find a different place to bury your bones, or whatever you're putting into the ground."

Dog just playfully nipped at her face and licked her all over.

She put Dog down and walked towards the door, with Dog at her heels. "No, you have to stay outside." He whimpered and turned his head to the side. Whining, he made it clear that he wanted a human to play with him. He wasn't going to give up that easily. Giving Taylour the saddest looking face ever, Dog waited. Taylour gave him a sidelong look, and then laughed at him. Picking him up, she brought him inside and up to her room.

As she tried on several combinations of skirts and sweaters and dresses and pants, she finally settled on a forest green wool sweater and a silver, knee-length pleated skirt that accented all of her best parts. She twirled around the mirror a few times and liked what she saw. She went into her closet to find the perfect shoes and found Dog wrestling with a pair.

"Hey, gimme those. Bad dog, Dog!" He growled at her, so she had to pick him up and pry his teeth off the shoes before he finally let go. He wiggled free and immediately went for another pair, but she shooed him out of the room with her foot and closed the door. She put earrings on and a pearl necklace, and then left.

Dog was in the hallway chewing on one of Spencer's shoes -- "Not my dog, not my problem" -- but he followed Taylour down the stairs as she left the house.

The Fallen Body

Keeping him outside was key to the survival of any of the other shoes in the house, so she let him scamper off.

She got into her car and drove to the restaurant, which was on the west side of downtown near the railroad tracks that bisected Marlinsville. Prairie House was an old lumber mill that had been converted into a steak house. Now it had a western theme, with stuffed bison, antelope and deer heads mounted on the walls. Old lanterns with candles inside were used to light the individual tables. Taylour grabbed her briefcase, exited the car, and strolled up to the entrance. The hostess took her name and directed her to a private booth.

She instructed the hostess to bring Mr. Philip Davidson back when he arrived.

Taylour glanced at her phone to see the time and saw that it was 7:03 p.m. The restaurant was filling up fast, so they were lucky to already have a place to sit. She peered around the corner of the booth and saw Philip just as he was entering, so she motioned for him to come over to her booth.

They shook hands, which made Taylour blush and Philip shift his feet before sitting down. They exchanged a few pleasantries and the waitress took their orders. Once they were alone, Taylour got down to business.

"How is Sarah adjusting to her new friend? Karen, isn't it?"

"Oh, they're fine. They have actually hit it off. They know exactly when to talk about things and when to leave each other to their own thoughts."

"And how is the investigation going?"

"I got some information from a friend up in New Jersey. Apparently, there may be ties to the Russian mafia that we are still investigating."

The Fallen Body

Taylour paused to take a sip of her Diet Coke. "Something interesting happened a few days ago." She recounted the events surrounding Betty's sudden disappearance. "Does that sound like something the Russian mafia might do?"

"It is. They throw money around, buying people off in exchange for information or favors. I'm concerned that she hasn't returned your calls."

"You don't think anything has happened to her, do you?"

Philip shrugged. "Can't say for sure."

Taylour stared at her drink. They were not making a whole lot of progress.

"Have you heard anything from the private investigator that you hired in New Jersey?"

"Not a word, which makes me irritated."

"Do you want me to look into it?"

"Nah, I got it covered."

"And Betty? Do you want me to see what I can find out about her?"

Taylour shrugged. "It wouldn't hurt to know what was going on there."

Their food was brought to them, so they dug in. As they ate, Taylour told funny stories about her past clients and Philip shared anecdotes of being a Texas Ranger. Their conversation flowed easily, and Taylour found herself enjoying Philip's companionship. It had been a long time for her where she actually talked with a man about topics that interested her.

Finally, after turning down dessert, the bill was placed on the table. Despite her earlier statement about letting him spring for dinner, she offered to pay for her meal, but Philip would have none of that.

"Alright, I agree to let you pay, but in exchange, I want one thing."

Philip squirmed, but managed to give her a half-smile. "And what is that?"

"When this is all done, I want you to take me on a real date, with dancing and my choice of restaurants, OK?"

Laughing out loud, Philip said, "Taylour, I look forward to that."

Chapter 35

Taylour slammed the phone down in frustration. Her phone calls to the private investigator in New Jersey were going unanswered, and she was now beyond irritation.

There it was again. That lure of working for a prestigious law firm. That burning desire to tangle with the big boys on a significant case. She longed to work for a company that valued her skills as a litigator. A place where she didn't have to be her own paralegal, where someone else answered the phone. Where clients respected her time and showed up at their scheduled appointments instead of just barging in unannounced. Where people returned your phone calls.

She sat back in her chair, her fingers in a pyramid shape touching her mouth. While she still felt a twinge in her arm, she no longer wore her sling. *It was getting in the way.* After ruminating for several minutes about what her options where, she pushed herself away from her desk. She pinched her lips together and called out to Spencer.

"Spencer, I need to get on the next flight out of Dallas/Ft. Worth to Newark. Can you make those arrangements and send them to my phone?"

The Fallen Body

"Why are you going to New Jersey, boss?"

"I need to connect with my private eye that I hired up there. Something is not right."

"Sure thing."

She stuffed several files in her briefcase that she could work on during the flight and dropped off a to-do list for Spencer. "If I get any calls of an urgent nature, patch them through to my cell phone. Otherwise, tell them that I'll return in a couple of days. There are the usual filings, so you can deliver those to the court and arrange for a process server to serve what is necessary." While Betty was invaluable in the office, she never wanted to serve legal papers, so they always had to hire someone to do that. With Spencer, he was eager to do that and had already signed up for a class to certify himself as a process server.

"Spencer, I am really quite proud of what you have accomplished in such a short period of time. You took over running the place when Betty disappeared, you organized the entire office so that things are actually in their place, and you got up to speed on what open cases we have."

Spencer grinned from ear to ear. "Yeah, well, I just needed to be given a chance to prove myself."

"Well, I am impressed at what you have done. Send me those details on my flight when you get them, OK?"

"You bet. I'll walk home when I'm done here."

"About that, I've been thinking that you need a better mode of transportation. How about we talk about that when I get back. You definitely deserve something better than simply coming to the office when I do."

Spencer's eyes perked up. "That would be awesome, thanks, Taylour!"

The Fallen Body

Taylour left the office and swung by the house to get an overnight bag. After packing a few things, she headed north, out of town. She did not run into any traffic on the way until she reached the edge of the Dallas/Ft. Worth metroplex. She had received a text from Spencer along the way with her trip information, so she drove her car straight to the DFW airport. Her American flight didn't leave until four o'clock that afternoon, but Taylour did not want to take any chances, so she took the shorter route through Ft. Worth, north on I-820, and then north on Hwy 121. Once at the airport, she headed towards Terminal A and parked her car.

Since she was not checking any bags, she went right up to the check-in counter and got her boarding pass. Forty five minutes later, the airplane taxied to the runway and she was on her way.

Taylour managed to get a little bit of work done while in the air, but she started to get sleepy, so she closed her laptop and decided to take a little nap. While most people find it hard to sleep on planes, Taylour had learned a long time ago how to shut her body down when it came time for rest, especially when she was tired, and she was exhausted. She took her jacket, curled it up for a pillow, and slept soundly for the rest of the flight.

After landing, she retrieved her carry-on bag and purse, and then rented a car. She pulled out an address that she had jotted down before she left her office. Using the GPS on her phone, she navigated her way to the Newark docks.

Once she found the location of the private eye's office, she pulled up and parked her car. There was a lone light that hung over the door, giving off a feeble glow, so she got out. The smell of diesel fuel and sea salt assailed her nose as she breathed in. As she looked around, the lights of the Port of Newark twinkled across the waterfront. Beyond the port, the lights of Lower Manhattan reflected off of the clouds overhead, giving her a sense of foreboding, as if a storm was about to roll through.

She pounded on the door, shouting, "Pierre! Are you in there?" Not seeing any vehicles parked in the vicinity, she tried the door. It was locked. She reached into her purse to pull out her tension wrench and pick. She gently applied pressure in the cylinder with the tension wrench while she inserted the pick towards the back. She raked the pick from back to front, and as she pushed the lower pins up, she heard the soft clicks as the upper pins set itself on the outside of the cylinder. Once all of the upper pins were set, she turned the tension wrench and the lock was released.

Taylour pushed the heavy door open and let it shut behind her. The darkness of the room engulfed her as she dug out her flashlight. She turned it on and swept it over the room. Not seeing any windows that would give any interior lights away to any passers-by, she found the switch and flipped it on.

The room was clean, too clean. There was not a speck of dirt or lint on the cement floor or the area rug that was placed in front of the desk. Even the artificial tree was free of dust on the faded leaves. She went over to the computer and turned it on, but nothing came up. Frustrated, she panned her eyes over the room. She noticed a small broom closet off towards the back of the room, so she went over to it and pulled it open.

She screamed when a dead body tumbled out and landed with a thud on the hard floor in front of her. She turned and stumbled to the front door, but then the door burst open and several police, with their guns pointed forward and their flashlights sweeping the room, filed in, one after another.

"Federal agents, hands in the air!"

Taylour jumped back and threw her hands in the air. *Not again!* She froze in place and allowed the SWAT team to push past her. One of them grabbed her hands and cuffed them, but she resisted and said, "Get your hands off of me, I'm not a criminal."

The leader gave a signal to the SWAT member to back off. He gave her a hard stare and said through his teeth, "Then what are you doing with a dead body in your closet?"

"This is not my office, and I only just saw that body before you came barreling through that door. How did you manage to show up at exactly the same time that I discovered it?"

"We received an anonymous tip about this place about an hour ago. We heard a scream, so we forced our way in. Who are you, anyway?"

"I'm Taylour Dixxon, and I'm a lawyer in Texas. I hired that man," she pointed at the corpse, "to investigate one of my cases, and when I didn't hear back from him, I came up here to find out what was going on."

"Does finding out what was going on include breaking and entering, Ms. Dixxon?"

Taylour blushed, but she held her ground. "I know this doesn't look good, but you can verify my story with Philip Davidson, who is a Texas R--"

"I know who Philip Davidson is. I talked to him a few days ago." He rubbed his mouth and chin. "You're Sarah Cockrell Baines' lawyer, aren't you." When she nodded, he introduced himself. "The name's Marco Borelli."

The Fallen Body

The FBI agent pulled out his badge to show it to Taylour, and then ushered her over to the sofa while he sat behind the desk. He shifted in his seat before he started.

"We have been investigating a man named Dmitri Polzin, who is reputed to be involved in the Russian Mafia, specifically as a brigadier for one of the bosses, called a *pakhan*. After Davidson called, we went to retrieve the write up on him and found a few more pieces to the puzzle. Come to find out that a Mr. Neal Baines was an attorney for a witness that was preparing to testify against Polzin. When the witness discovered that Mr. Baines had been murdered, she disappeared. Fell completely off of the grid. Before Davidson called, we didn't understand the connection between Polzin and the disappearance of our witness."

Taylour's mouth dropped and she gave Agent Borelli an incredulous stare.

"So now we are concerned that Polzin may be looking for your client, Sarah Baines. Have you had any threats or unusual activity surrounding her case?"

"Um, er, well..." Taylour weighed in her mind whether or not the sudden departure of Betty was connected. "Since we are in the mode of sharing information, I do have one concern." She related the recent events surrounding Betty, including the letter that she found about taking care of her gambling debts. "I'm not sure that they are related, but her leaving on such short notice was a bit startling. Now she won't return my calls and seems to have disappeared."

Agent Borelli slapped the side of his leg and pointed his finger for emphasis. "That is *exactly* the kinda thing that Polzin can pull off. He, or someone that works for him, could have easily found out about the gambling debt

The Fallen Body

and promised to make it evaporate if she disappeared for a while."

"So, your saying that this Polzin--"

"Or someone who worked for Polzin."

"--Is trying to find Sarah? Why would he do that? Sarah was arrested for her husband's murder, but was released. If she had been tried and found guilty, then he wouldn't have anything to worry about."

"It doesn't make any sense if Sarah is oblivious to the connection between Mr. Baines and Polzin, but it makes perfect sense if she is somehow involved with Polzin, or someone working for Polzin, and he wants to keep tabs on her. He might even want to see what she knows about him."

Taylour threw up her hands. "So, you're telling me that my client may still be involved in her husband's murder, but may not be the actual murderer, right?"

Agent Borelli paused, and then chose his next words carefully. "There are still suspicions surrounding your client. Right now, the safest place for her is in protective custody. If Polzin comes after her, he is going to find it difficult."

"Agent Borelli, I'm not sure that I believe you. My client was recently attacked *while* in prison. She wasn't safe there. As it stands now, this Polzin dude may be coming after me!"

"Ms. Dixxon, I understand your concerns. We have those same concerns for your safety. However, we are not convinced yet that Ms. Baines is innocent. Her fingerprints were all over the murder weapon. She certainly had one of two motives. Either she was completely oblivious to her husband's dealings with his client and suspected him of having an affair, or she is tied to Polzin and was complicit in his death. Either way, she stays in protective custody, at least for the time being."

Taylour clutched her stomach and shook her head back and forth. She put a quivering hand to her forehead and slumped back into her seat. "This is too much. I-I need to go."

"Where are you going?"

"I need to clear my head. Do you know any nice beaches where I can just become an anonymous tourist, without a care in the world except whether to sleep on the beach or get a nice massage?"

Agent Borelli chuckled. "I know how you feel sometimes. Always chasing bad guys, never giving up on catching them, and then starting over the next day and the next."

Taylour looked up at Agent Borelli with a smile after glancing at the ring on his finger. "Look, Agent Borelli, I need to get back to Texas. I have several other clients to take care of. If you don't mind, I will be on my way."

Special Agent Marco Borelli handed Taylour his business card and told her to contact him if she needed anything. She thanked him and left in her rental car.

Heading back to the airport, she decided that she needed to talk with Philip about what was going on. This case was perplexing, notwithstanding all the information that she had received tonight from the FBI. She was dedicated to helping her client in any way that she could, and right now, she believed that keeping Sarah in protective custody for the time being might be the best and safest option for her.

Chapter 36

Taylour spent the rest of the week catching up on her other cases and had no spare time to think about Sarah's situation. At night, she was either attending a board meeting of the Marlinsville Literary Foundation, or she was so completely exhausted that she came home and went straight to bed. By Friday morning she was all caught up, with only a few appointments that afternoon.

She tapped the end of her pen on her desk as she ruminated about Pierre Fontanot. Why someone would want him dead. Did he leave any clues behind? What had he found out about her case that would spook someone bad enough to have him killed? Her head was spinning from all the possibilities.

Finally, just before lunch, she called out, "Spencer, can you get Philip Davidson on the phone?"

"Sure thing, boss," came the muffled reply from up front.

A moment passed, and then Spencer yelled, "He's on line one."

Taylour snatched up the phone and said, "We need to talk."

The Fallen Body

A chuckle came through the line. "Not even a 'Howdy' from you, or 'How are things'?"

Taylour smiled. "Sorry, I forget those pleasantries when I am focused."

"I'll say. So, does this request to meet come with any expectations on my part?"

Taylour blushed. "Sorry, I didn't mean to come on too strong. I just thought that we should touch base again with regards to Sarah. It can't be easy for her, putting her life on hold while we try to figure out who killed her husband."

"I agree. However, I am prepared to change the arrangement somewhat, if that's OK with you."

"What do you mean, change the arrangement?"

"Since nothing of concern seems to have popped up since we whisked her away, and because the protective order has expired, maybe she can stay at her Aunt Edna's house. If she is willing to pay for it, she can hire a bodyguard service if she feels threatened."

"OK. That is different than what Borelli told me earlier. What changed?"

"Let's talk about that over dinner. You game?"

"Do you mean tonight?" She sat up straight, suddenly nervous.

Philip chuckled. "Of course. And we can go dancing afterwards, as promised previously."

"So, this is a date, right?"

"It could be more, if that's what you want."

"Now look who's coming on strong." Taylour laughed as she twirled a strand of hair through her fingers. She gave him the details to Tortilla Casa.

"I'll see you tonight at six thirty, then."

Taylour caught herself smiling as she thought about what might happen after tonight's dancing. She only allowed her fantasies to run wild for a moment before she forced herself back to work.

The afternoon consisted of client consultations about estate planning, title work, and some community development projects for the town. By 5 o'clock, Taylour was ready to call it a day. She went home, took a quick shower, and was ready to go by 6:15. She hopped in her car and sped off.

Chapter 37

A black Yukon followed her to the restaurant, and Roman observed her enter and take a seat at her favorite spot by the window in the far corner. A scowl crossed his face.

Roman reached into a bag behind him and got out of the car, strolling nonchalantly to the back of the restaurant. He had an idea. He approached one of the cooking staff who was taking a smoking break.

"Hey, *muchacho,* how would you like to earn a hundred bucks?"

The Mexican looked around, saw no one, and said, "What do you want, *gringo?*" He dropped his cigarette butt and grounded it into the pavement with his foot.

Roman pulled out a 100-dollar bill and gave him a hard grin. "This can be yours if you do me a small favor. What is your name?"

"Miguel."

Moving towards him, Roman said, "Miguel, do you know who Ms. Dixxon is? She seems to be a regular here."

The Fallen Body

Leaning back and folding his arms, Miguel responds, "*La guapa* with the reddish blonde hair? Yeah, I know her. I just saw her sit down at her favorite table."

Roman pulled out a small, non-descript bottle. "I want you to sprinkle a little of this on her order, and then throw it away in the trash."

Miguel squinted furtively at Roman, then at the money. His eyes shot down to his feet and he said, "Two-hundred."

"You will get the other hundred if you bring the bottle back to me."

Hesitant at first, then with determination on his face, Miguel grabbed both the bottle and the cash at the same time. He stuffed the cash in his front pocket, palmed the bottle, and then whirled around to go back inside.

* * *

Miguel hid the bottle behind some Styrofoam cups. He looked out from the kitchen and saw Taylour stand up to greet Philip as he entered in a rush, pecking him on the cheek before they both sat down opposite of each other. Taylour's cheeks turned red from her greeting, but he acted as if he didn't notice. The waitress appeared just at that moment to take their drink orders – one diet Coke with a lemon and one raspberry lemonade – and then bustled off to give them time to look over the menu.

From where they were sitting, Miguel could see the two of them as they leaned imperceptibly towards each other. When the gentleman said something that made Ms. Dixxon laugh, Miguel drew his mouth into a straight line and bit his lip.

Miguel could feel the searing heat from the oven as he moved around to fill the orders. He noticed sweat roll down his cheeks, so he brushed the sides of his face with his sleeves. He felt thirsty and tugged at his clothes. He

The Fallen Body

kept his eyes open for the order from table 13, and when he saw the order for two chicken enchiladas and another order for beef fajitas, he made a snap decision.

As he assembled Taylour's food order, he called for the other cook, "*Me agarra algunos pollo del congelador, por favor,*" (Grab me some chicken from the freezer, please). When he was alone, he snatched the bottle from its hiding place and took off the lid. His fumbling fingers dropped the top and it rolled out of reach under the oven. Leaving it behind, he lightly shook the bottle over the chicken in the enchiladas. He mixed the light gray powdery substance in with the meat, finished making the rest of the enchilada, and called for the plate to be delivered with the beef fajitas that Philip ordered.

Miguel dropped to the ground in search of the lid, saw it just out of reach, and frantically grabbed a spatula to help push it over to the side, but could not reach it. He heard the cook coming back, so he lunged with the spatula, which pushed the lid out into view. He scrambled on his knees to retrieve it, hastily screwing it back on the bottle. When the top was secure, he pushed past the surprised cook and stumbled towards the back door.

He shuffled over to Roman and handed him the bottle without saying a word, his eyes darting left and right.

Roman, enjoying the discomfort of the man, slapped him soundly on the shoulder with his big hand, clenched Miguel with a tight, steely clasp, and said, "Well done, *amigo.*" Roman opened up the container of arsenic and noted that Miguel had used about a third of the poison. He pulled out a hundred dollar bill, stuffed it in Miguel's front pocket, and pivoted back to his vehicle. Miguel gulped, snatched the cash from his front pocket and ran back inside, stuffing the bill in his pants pocket.

The Fallen Body

* * *

"So, what did the principal do when he found his car?" Philip asked.

Inside the restaurant, it was starting to get crowded. Taylour looked around and saw younger couples out on a date mixed with moms, dads and their little children. Grandparents smiled and chatted with their grandchildren about school activities, sports, and the latest gossip going around. Laughter and conversation, combined with the Tejano music being piped in through the speakers, made it difficult to have a conversation.

Philip and Taylour were in the middle of sharing hilarious stories about their past, specifically the craziest stunts and practical jokes that they had pulled off while in high school and college. Taylour had just finished recounting the time that their senior class moved the principal's Volkswagen Bug from the parking lot to the football field, turned it upside down, and decorated it with shaving cream and toilet paper.

"He was livid! The next morning he made an announcement over the intercom system that our graduation ceremony was going to be canceled unless the perpetrators came forward and confessed."

After they received their food from their waitress, Taylour grabbed her fork and knife, cut into the enchiladas, and stabbed at the chicken. She was just about to stick the bite into her mouth when she was accidentally bumped from behind and her fork flew out of her hand.

"Oh, I'm so sorry!" said the older gentleman who had bumped Taylour. "I don't think that I have ever seen it this crowded before! Forgive my clumsiness."

Taylour smiled back at him and accepted his apologies. She picked up her fork, but just before she was going to put it into her mouth, she squinted at it. The chicken appeared to be a bit more gray than usual. *That's odd.* She put it to her nose and sniffed. The familiar aroma of grilled chicken filled her nose as the spices permeated through her.

"Is there something wrong?" Philip asked.

Taylour shrugged her shoulders and said, "Nah, everything is fine." She took the bite and chewed.

"Well, the way that you were looking at your food, you would have thought that someone was trying to poison—"

Taylour spat out the enchilada and flew up from the table. She shoved her way through the crowd, holding back the nausea, stumbling past the sign that said "*Caballeros*," and through the door for the "*Damas.*"

She yanked open a stall door and fell to the floor, her head over the porcelain. She heaved and coughed until she had nothing left, and then dry heaved for good measure. She pushed her hair over her ear with the back of her hand and stood up on shaky legs. She staggered over to the sink and turned the cold water on. The coolness of the water felt soothing on her face and cheeks as she splashed the liquid over her. She snatched a paper towel, got it wet, and dabbed it on the back of her neck.

"Taylour? Are you alright?" She heard Philip's muffled voice from outside. She wobbled uneasily over to the door and almost fainted from the effort.

"I'm OK, I just had, uh, something *unpleasant* happen."

"Was it something that you ate? If that's the case, let me speak with the owner."

"No, no. I mean, yes, it was something that I ate, but there is no need to get the owner."

Taylour pushed open the door to exit. Philip reached out his hand to steady her as Taylour was as white as a ghost. She grasped his arm and let him guide her to the nearest chair, which was right on the edge of the dining area. Taylour felt embarrassed at the stares that she was getting from the patrons, so she mustered her energy and motioned for Philip to take her outside.

She staggered to the nearest place to sit, which was occupied by a white-haired lady in her 60's. When she saw Taylour with her disheveled hair and pale visage, she quickly stood up and offered her the seat. Taylour thanked her as she collapsed onto the wooden bench.

Philip thanked the lady as well and asked her to get Taylour a glass of water from inside. He sat next to Taylour, holding her hands to keep them warm, and inquired as to how she was feeling. A glass of water was handed to her and she gulped it down, pausing only to take a breath before finishing it off.

A crowd started forming around them, and while everyone's attention was focused on the lady who apparently ate something that disagreed with her, Miguel made his way to her table and cleared her poisoned plate before someone could figure out what happened. He dumped the toxic food in the garbage can and placed her plate with all of the other stacked dirty dishes that had not made it yet through the dishwasher. He then sauntered back to the kitchen and breathed a sigh of relief.

As the color started coming back to Taylour's cheeks, her ears turned red at the attention she was getting, so she glanced around for an escape and stood up shakily. She waved off Philip's offer for help and started slowly towards her car.

"I suppose that a night of dancing is out of the question," she joked.

The Fallen Body

Philip suppressed a smile and said, "You are one tough lady, Taylour Dixxon. You just had food poisoning and yet, here you are making wisecracks." He shook his head and then peered into her red eyes. "There isn't a lot that can faze you, is there?"

Taylour chuckled. "I guess not. But don't think for a single moment that you have gotten out of going dancing with me. Will you take a rain check?"

"Do I have a choice?"

"Why, Philip, are you implying that you don't have any control over whether or not you go out with me? Especially since I have made such a spectacle of myself this evening."

Philip laughed out loud this time. He stammered out a reply. "I'm not sure that you should be left alone with all that just happened. Are you sure that you don't need me to keep you company?"

She felt an instant yearning for his companionship, and almost changed her mind, but she held firm. "I really just need to lie down and then I'll be fine in the morning. I appreciate your offer, though." She bit her lower lip, and then asked, "Are you going to be in town tomorrow?"

Philip shook his head. "I need to get back. My business here is done."

"Pity. I'll call you tomorrow then, OK? We still have things to discuss."

Philip helped Taylour get into her car, and she rolled the window down to say goodbye. He leaned in and kissed her lightly on the cheek, but bumped the back of his head when he withdrew, which caused them both to laugh.

The Fallen Body

"At least I'm leaving on a good note," Taylour said as she rolled her window up. She waved at him and he stared at her as she drove off.

Chapter 38

As soon as Taylour made it home, she went straight to bed, the effects of the food poisoning having completely wiped her out. She slept late the next morning.

With the direct light from the sun brightening her bedroom, she reached her hand out from under the covers, turned the alarm clock to where she could see it, and then groaned when she saw 10:58 a.m. staring at her.

She needed to run, to sweat out the aches and pains from the previous night's adventures, so she got dressed in her workout clothes and jogged about three miles around her normal circuit. The air had lost all its crispness and was just warm, but that was exactly what she needed to sweat as she ran along the side of the highway. However, just a mile into her jog, the acrid smell of decomposition assailed her nostrils from not-so-fresh road kill. It was either a raccoon or an armadillo -- not a skunk, luckily -- so she ran wide of those carcasses. She peered into the sky for buzzards, but didn't see a single one circling overhead.

As she ran, she turned over in her mind what happened at the restaurant. That had never happened before, and she prided herself on having an iron stomach. Maybe she was getting old and having to take antacids with her meals. Pfft! That wasn't it.

Taylour tried to remember more details about that night, but all she could remember was the comfortable conversation that she was having with Philip. His self-deprecating humor had made her laugh more than once, and she found herself wishing that she could have gone dancing with him as planned.

After she finished with her run, Taylour and Spencer did some much needed chores around the house.

She also needed to talk with Philip about Sarah. She called him on his phone, but he didn't answer right away.

It wasn't until lunch time that he responded to her call. He explained to Taylour that, in light of her recent bout with food poisoning, that it might be prudent to put Taylour in protective custody with Sarah.

"There is no way that I can do that. I have too many responsibilities to be putting my life on hold like that."

"Taylour, I know that you think you can take care of yourself, but please reconsider." Philip paused to clear his throat. "I don't want anything to happen to you."

Taylour smiled, but held firm. In the end, they decided to ask Sarah what she wanted to do. Did she want to continue in protective custody? Or did she feel safe enough to stay by herself in her aunt's house. The two of them would touch base again in a few days.

At the end of the day, Taylour and Spencer were both too exhausted to do anything else, so they cleaned themselves up and went to bed.

Chapter 39

The following Tuesday, Taylour groaned when she realized that she had a follow-up appointment with Mr. Greer at 11 o'clock.

Nathaniel Greer was not someone that Taylour particularly liked, but he was rich and he paid his bills on time. He owned the largest feed store in town, Greer's Goods, and he constantly reminded people about it. He had used Taylour's legal services sporadically in the past, but he had hinted on using her office exclusively and had arranged to meet with her privately at her office today to discuss business.

Taylour stumbled through her morning routine, still feeling the residual effects from her brush with death, and was out the door by 10:30. She arrived at her office and noticed that there was a black Cadillac Deville parked in front of her office in the handicapped parking spot. Groaning again, she gathered her briefcase and sweater and slammed her car door. Mr. Greer was early.

She opened the door to her office, said hello to Spencer, but didn't see Mr. Greer. Spencer mouthed the words, "He's in your office," and made a face, which did not bode well for the meeting she was about to have. She

The Fallen Body

hung her coat, went to the kitchen, and pulled out a Gatorade from the refrigerator. Leaning up against the counter, she waited. Looking at her watch on her wrist, she twisted the cap back onto her bottle and placed the drink back into the fridge. She paced back and forth several times before she summoned up the courage to walk into her office.

She breezed past Mr. Greer as he said, "Ms. Dixxon, I have a problem, and I need your help."

She put on a smile, reached out her hand, and said, "Good morning, Mr. Greer. How are you doing today?"

Mr. Greer paused, and then shook her hand. It was clammy and he didn't even bother to squeeze back. "How do you think I'm doing? I need a lawyer, that's how I'm doing."

Taking a deep breath and letting it out slowly, Taylor leaned back in her chair and assessed the man in front of her. He was in his late 50's, about 5' 7", nearly bald, with the physique of Santa Claus without the mirth. Children have a keen sense of intuition about people, whether they are pleasant or mean, naughty or nice, and Taylour had no doubts that if any child was placed on Mr. Greer's lap, they would run screaming to their mother.

Taylour shook her head ever so slightly to clear her thoughts and asked, "What can I do for you today?"

Instead of answering, Mr. Greer got up and started pacing back and forth. "Anything that I tell you is in confidence, right? Even though I haven't paid you anything yet?"

Taylour didn't miss a beat. "Yes, of course. As we talked about over the phone earlier, you have retained my services in the past, so that makes you a client of mine. Everything that we say is in total confidence."

The Fallen Body

"And anything that I might have said to your receptionist, or anything that he might overhear," he motioned with his head, "that is also in confidence, right?"

"Of course, Mr. Greer." Taylour crossed her arms and clenched her jaw. She wanted to reach across the desk and wring his neck, but she controlled herself.

"Well, what I'm about to tell you could get me in a lot of trouble." He hurriedly sat down and turned away from facing Taylour directly.

Nodding, but tightly, Taylour said, "Go on."

"I want to start by saying that it has been hard since my wife, ah, left me last year. She and I argued about this and that, nothing big that I thought we couldn't work out. When she served me with divorce papers, I just lost it. I begged her to come back, told her that I would change. I was even willing to seek counseling, which is a big deal for me, y'know?

"Anyway, she took off and I was lonely." He shifted in his chair, not able to find a comfortable spot, so he jumped up again and walked back and forth, this time with more agitation. "I, uh, started going on Internet chat sites, y'know, to let off some steam. I found it very easy to pretend to be someone else, like a 24 year old architect designing an art museum, or a doctor just finishing his residency. I even tried my hand at being a younger woman," he puffed, "but that didn't go to well, so I stuck to being a man, albeit a younger version of me."

Taylour sensed where this was heading, but she remained quiet as she jotted down some notes.

Nathaniel continued, "I started chatting with this girl who said she was 18. She said that she was going to graduate from high school this year and that she lived in Arlington, TX, so I told her that I was a junior at nearby

The Fallen Body

TCU. We hit it off immediately. I mean, we could talk about anything. I could tell that she was lonely, just like me, and so we arranged to meet at a restaurant in downtown Fort Worth. We both like seafood, so we decided on Daddy Jack's on Throckmorton. She told me her name was Allison, and I told her I was David. No last names, not until we met."

"Weren't you worried that she would be upset when she found out that you weren't a college student?"

"Of course, I'm not stupid. She told me she was going to wear a black skirt and a white Cardigan sweater with a red rose pin, so I told her that I was going to be dressed in a dark blue blazer with a white carnation on my lapel. We were going to meet at 7 p.m. Instead, I went at 6:30 in jeans and a sweatshirt and sat near the door so that I could watch as she came in."

Taylour flinched. "So, what happened after that?"

Nathaniel sat down in the chair again and stared straight at Taylour. "I waited, and sure enough, Allison showed up at five minutes to seven. She had done her hair up real nice, with curls just like my wife used to do, and when she walked past me, she smelled like jasmine. The waitress guided her to a table and she looked around expectantly. She was so beautiful and young! I felt my cheeks get warm, and, uh, well, I suddenly got very nervous. How was I going to handle this? She looked so vulnerable, so pretty, and I didn't want to disappoint her, but at the same time, I felt so inferior, so self-conscious.

"I had a perfect view of her from where I was sitting, and she had no idea that I was the one that she had come to see. Whenever the door opened, she would turn to see if it was David, and every time it wasn't David, she would bite her lower lip in disappointment. After about 15 minutes, she started fidgeting. She was always glancing at her cell phone to see what time it was. I felt so sorry for her. At about 7:30, I could see tears forming in her eyes, and I watched her as they ran down her face. I couldn't stand it any longer, so I slowly stood up and walked over to her table and sat down.

"At first she was confused, so when I told her that I was David, she stuttered and ran her hand through her hair. I talked to her in a calm voice and apologized for deceiving her, but that she looked so lovely and pretty, I had to explain to her the truth. I thought that I could get her to understand what I had done, and I hoped that she would just laugh it off and then confide in me and that everything would be just the way it was before when we were chatting. But instead, she got real mad and jumped up from the table."

Taylour stopped writing and narrowed her eyes at him. He looked so pathetic and old and creepy as he recounted his story. How else did he think she was going to react? Taylour shivered, and then motioned for Mr. Greer to continue.

"I went after her and caught up with her in the parking lot. I pleaded with her to forgive me. She whirled around at me with such loathing and hatred in her eyes that I stopped dead in my tracks. She told me that she was only 16 and that she knew that this had been a mistake and that she had snuck out of her mom's house without her knowing and that she was going to be in so much trouble when she got home. I tried to calm her by placing my hand on her arm, but she wouldn't let me touch her, she wouldn't let me comfort her."

He paused for a moment and ran his hand over his eyes as if he was trying to squeeze out what he had seen at that particular moment. "I hugged her tight, and when she struggled to get loose, I could tell that she was about

The Fallen Body

to scream, to yell, so I placed my hand over her mouth and held it there, just held it there. Her eyes bore into me, and I fell deep into them as I held her. I could tell that she loved me at that very moment. Her blue eyes were so passionate and full of life and moist, so I hugged her tighter and said over and over to her, "I love you too," and "I know that you love me," and "we will always be together."

Taylour's hand flew to her mouth as she suppressed a shriek. She was frozen in place and missed his next words. "What? What did you just say?"

"I said, the light in her eyes went out, just like that." He snapped his fingers. "I let her go, bit by bit, and shook her to try and revive her, but she wouldn't wake up."

Silence filled the room. Taylour pretended to take notes, but she couldn't focus on the paper. This man just recounted to her how he snuffed the life out of a girl. Taylour finally forced herself to look at him. The pathetic creature could not look in her direction. He was in front of her, yet Taylour could tell that he did not want to be there.

"Mr. Greer, what did you do after that?" Taylour managed to whisper, trying as hard as she could to remain calm and professional.

"Well, as soon as I realized what I had done, I dragged her body so that it was out of view. I placed her gently on the slope of the hill that was behind the parking lot, and then I left. I got in my car and drove back here to Marlinsville."

Taylour composed herself and started asking questions. When did this happen? (Four or five days ago). Did anyone see you in the parking lot? (I don't think so).

The Fallen Body

Did you try anything to revive her? (I shook her a couple of times, but other than that, no).

She stopped with her notes. She turned to her computer and searched for any news stories related to this attack. She found something, clicked on it, and read it silently. Her eyes perked up as she read that a 16 year old girl by the name of Allison (last name not revealed because she was a minor) had been attacked in the parking lot of Daddy Jack's, had lost consciousness, but was revived by a Good Samaritan who happened across her body. The hero was a 26 year old named Jack Boyce, a student at Texas Wesleyan.

"Allison was taken to a nearby hospital, where, except for a tiny case of amnesia, she is expected to make a full recovery."

Mr. Greer perked up. "What did you say? She didn't die? What a relief!"

He practically leapt from his chair and was on his way out of her office when a disbelieving Taylour called him back in and ordered him to sit down. He did so reluctantly.

Taylour threw her hands in the air. "Do you somehow think that you are no longer in trouble, Mr. Greer?"

He stared at a spot on the floor.

"You are still in a bad way. My advice to you is to either come clean to the police, or be willing to offer a lot of money to this Allison girl. You are lucky that there don't appear to be any physical effects of your attack."

"Attack? I didn't attack her! I… I love her. I was trying to get her to listen to me, to understand me. I didn't want to hurt her, and since she's OK, I don't see what the big deal is."

The Fallen Body

Refusing to look at him, Taylour said, "While there may not be physical injuries, there most certainly will be psychological damage that will need to be repaired. My goodness, you nearly suffocated her!"

Finally, she turned to face him, her finger in his face. "And you will *fix* that, won't you, Mr. Greer?" With her eyebrows lowered and pinched together, she stalked out of the office before he could respond and went straight to the office restroom. She slammed the door behind her, locked it, and rushed over to the sink to splash some cool water on her face. She shuddered as she thought about how she had been in the same room as Mr. Greer. She heard the office door close faintly as Mr. Greer left, so she unlocked the door and poked her head out.

"He's gone, Taylour." Spencer said from the front. She heard the phone ring and Spencer answered it without missing a beat. His voice carried down the hallway as it pushed Taylour back into her office.

She closed the door softly, as if she intended to slowly drift away unannounced, with little fanfare. If she slammed the door, that would draw too much attention to herself, and "they" might come after her, to talk her out of leaving. This way, she could simply evaporate and no one would be the wiser.

She still had a long day ahead of her, but before she started back to work, she jotted down the contact information listed on the website and made a mental note to contact the 16 year old girl named Allison.

Chapter 40

As border collies go, Dog didn't look all that different from other dogs of that same breed. His fur was both black and white, with smaller puppy ears that laid flat against his head. The black covered both eyes and either side of the face and head, with the white color creating an hourglass shape on his face. The lighter color continued onto the front paws and forward half, with the black taking over the back half all the way down to the back feet, which turned white just like the front feet. Dog's longer hair made him look like a big ball of fluffy energy as he jumped and attacked anything that moved, especially the baby rattles that Spencer had purchased for $2.99 at Barb's Pet Store in town.

Dog had a certain intelligence that went beyond that of most canines. While all dogs can sense danger to some degree or another, Dog had an almost sixth sense when it came to reading individuals and their intentions. He could look at Taylour and know exactly how her day had been, and would slink out of sight if he sensed a bad mood. He could also tell when a human wanted to play with him, and would retrieve any ball or stick that was thrown for him, dropping the item at the feet of the thrower and looking longingly into their eyes in anticipation of another toss. He had inexhaustible energy, bounding from one item of interest to another. Taylour found that his energy picked her spirits up whenever they were down. He was a constant presence under her feet when she made dinner, always hoping that a scrap of food would fall to the ground for him to gobble up. Taylour found herself smiling at his antics and would occasionally "drop" a small cut of meat – usually a piece that was too fatty for her tastes – and would laugh at his insatiable appetite and patience.

When Taylour and Spencer were gone, Dog roamed outside. Spencer always kept a clean bowl full of water and a small bucket of food on the porch near the door, but Dog rarely spent any time lounging around. He took his job of protecting the house very seriously, and growled at any threat, actual or perceived. He would rarely bark unless there was a good reason. He loved to chase the endless array of squirrels that had taken up residence in the tall oak trees surrounding the property. The squirrels did not tolerate Dog and chattered their displeasure at him constantly from the safety of the treetops. He seemed to know exactly when they were on the ground rounding up acorns and would scamper after them as if to play, but they would have nothing to do with him. Taylour and Spencer laughed whenever they saw Dog chase after one of them, but nothing prepared them for what they saw one lazy evening.

Taylour and Spencer were sitting on the porch both wrapped up in their respective blankets, taking in the outdoors with long, deep breaths, when Dog decided that he was going to explore the base of the largest oak tree in the yard. There were a number of acorns on the ground, and that meant that the squirrels were out gathering.

The Fallen Body

When Dog took off to chase the half dozen squirrels, he fully expected them to scatter like they always did, and all of them did run off in every direction, except the biggest squirrel, who was affectionately named Bubba.

Taylour called him Bubba because he was a little more rotund than the other squirrels, as well as a bit slower both on his feet and with his wits. Apparently, Bubba had decided after the last humiliating scattering of squirrels that he was not going to take it anymore. So, instead of running away while Dog came barreling at him, Bubba perched on his hind legs, puffed up his chest, and tried to stare down Dog.

However, Dog's momentum as he flung himself towards the tree carried him directly at Bubba, and they collided together like a bowling ball hitting a bowling pin. Yelping and yapping, the two furry bodies tumbled end over end together until the laws of physics spun them apart. The first to come to their senses was Bubba, who, after shaking his head for a moment, decided that it was best for him to climb the tree. He wobbled over to the base of the tree and slowly inched his way up, grasping the bark with his claws, until he found a branch to hold him. Once he was safely out of reach, he chattered long and loud at Dog, who jumped and barked and twisted himself around the base of the tree until he was exhausted. When a panting Dog finally turned towards Spencer and Taylour, all he could see was the two of them whooping and hollering as they were rolling on the porch, guffawing and laughing at what they had just witnessed.

* * *

It was a chilly Friday morning, with the frost covering every exposed surface of the yard, when Taylour and Spencer left for the office. The sun had yet to peek

The Fallen Body

over the horizon as they drove off together. There was not a cloud in the sky, which meant that the sun would soon melt away the coldness that lay heavily over the scene.

Several minutes later, Dog ventured out of his wooden doghouse, ready to take on the adventures of a new day. With his thick fur, he barely felt the hardness of the ground as he scampered back and forth. He perked his head up as a car drove up, a Black Yukon that he had never seen before. The Yukon stopped and the door opened.

As Roman stepped out, Dog sniffed the air. It reeked of vodka and fish, very different and foreign from what he normally smelled, so he let forth a low growl and held his ground.

"Ah, what do we have here? A guard dog, eh?" Roman held out his hand for Dog to smell, but Dog let out a growl and slowly backed away. He yapped once, and then turned around as if to look for the humans who lived in the house behind him.

Suddenly, Dog felt himself lifted up off of the ground. He struggled to get loose, but the kicking and scratching of his legs had little effect on the large man's coat and gloves. Dog tried biting at whatever he could get his mouth on, but to no avail. He felt himself being squeezed and yelped in pain.

Snap! Roman let his grip go from the twisted head and it flopped unnaturally over his arm. He carried Dog to the porch and dumped the lifeless body at the foot of the door. As he wheeled away, he thought to himself that maybe this will get the message across. He climbed into the Yukon and slowly drove away.

* * *

The Fallen Body

As Taylour tumbled into the car at the end of a hard day at work, she avoided eye contact with Spencer. She pursed her lips and stared straight ahead as they drove down the road towards home.

"Look, Auntie Taylour, I'm sorry. I really am!" Spencer said in desperation. "You gotta believe me. I didn't mean to mess up your court date today."

Taylour sighed, but said nothing as she gripped the steering wheel hard.

"I mean, I forgot to change the schedule after the first call, and I meant to go back and change the calendar, but then you came in and asked me for the Denton file, and then Mrs. Larsen popped in unexpectedly, and the phone kept ringing off the hook. I just couldn't keep up."

Taylour sighed again and said, "How are we coming on our search for a paralegal?"

"Uh, well, we don't have anyone yet."

"Why not?"

Now it was Spencer's turn to look away. "I called the SOS Temporary Help Agency and asked them for applicants, but, uh, they haven't sent over any yet."

"Spencer, I pay you to be the office manager, and I expect that the office will run smoothly when I'm not there. Have you set up any interviews?"

Spencer fidgeted in his seat, and then turned to face Taylour. "I'm sorry, I will do better tomorrow. I'll get right on that. It's just..." He paused.

Taylour turned to look at him, and saw that Spencer was unable to hold her gaze in his, as if he was conflicted about something. They pulled up to the front of the house and stopped.

"It's just what?" she asked.

The Fallen Body

Spencer opened up his mouth to explain himself when he jerked his gaze towards the pile of fur on the porch. "Is that Dog?"

Taylour knew something was wrong when he jumped out of the car and Dog did not come running. He sprinted the last few yards and bounded up the porch. "Dog!!??"

Taylour was confused at first, but when she heard Spencer's long, plaintive wail, she recognized immediately that something was wrong. She whipped out her phone and frantically pushed the buttons to the sheriff's department.

She paced back and forth nervously as the phone rang. "Thank you for calling the --"

"Darlene, this is Taylour. Listen, I don't have a lot of time to explain, but I need you to get the sheriff out here ASAP. There's been an incident here at the house that he needs to see."

"Of course, Taylour, hon. Just one sec, OK?"

Taylour gripped her phone tight as she listened to the background noise. She heard the distinct clicking and static of the walkie-talkie as Darlene efficiently dispatched the sheriff to Taylour's location. Before Darlene could say that the sheriff was on his way, Taylour thanked her and slapped the phone shut.

As Taylour stood there frozen, she felt the pangs of grief start in her toes and wash over her like a terrible chill. She reached out her hand on the car to steady herself. Memories of her dead father invaded her mind, the lack of color in his face and the surprising coldness of his cheek as she kissed him goodbye at the memorial service held in his honor. But mostly she remembered her mother, lying in a hospital bed, as the nurse administered a sedative to help her relax. Her mother closed her eyes, took one last, long breath, and then she was absolutely still. Taylour remembered the sting of her own tears on her cheeks as the heart monitor was switched off, a harsh click that seemed out of place in the surreal moment. It's not easy to watch someone die, even in their sleep.

She wanted to go over to Spencer, who was rocking Dog in his lap as tears rolled down his face and mixed with Dog's matted fur. Dread crept into as she witnessed Spencer's emotions. There was someone who wanted to do her harm, and she wasn't prepared for that.

Taylour wiped her eyes and turned away from the scene.

Chapter 41

Roman was starting to get nervous, and when Roman gets nervous, bad things happen. Taylour's activities on the murder case were starting to uncover the tracks that he had so desperately tried to hide. While he still felt confident that the information that the private investigator that she had hired would remain hidden, he was becoming increasingly worried that her zealous pursuit of the truth would expose him. It was like pulling on a thread. If you pulled on it long and far enough, the knitting unravels.

So it was with Roman. While his monitoring of her office was not revealing where Sarah was, it was showing how close she was getting to the truth, and her dogged persistence made him angry. But he knew how to get people to back off, and that is what he wanted her to do.

As he had wandered around town in his black Yukon these past few weeks, he had noticed a pattern with Taylour's work habits. She would almost always be at her office by 8:30 every morning, and would only come back to her home for lunch, which she did on a fairly regular basis by 12:30 every afternoon. She would then go back to work until 5:30 or 6 at night, but sometimes

The Fallen Body

earlier, which was a bit more unpredictable. That gave him a window of opportunity in the morning to cause some serious damage.

Early Tuesday morning he drove to the local hardware store and bought two 5-gallon gasoline containers with cash. He then took them to the gas station at the opposite end of town from Taylour's farm and filled them up, this time using a gas card so as not to attract attention to himself with the cashier. He loaded the containers into the back of his vehicle and proceeded towards Dixxon Manor.

Since it was still only about 8 o'clock, he parked his car just down the road behind a tree and waited for Taylour and Spencer to drive past.

However, this was not a typical morning as she and Spencer had left already to go to work. As he sat in his car, she was already knee deep in legal briefs, continuances, etc.

As he stewed in his car, thinking that she was running late, it wasn't until 9:30 or so before he considered driving past her place of business to see if she was already there. Turning the car back on and slamming the gear into place, he sped down the road in order to pass by. Sure enough, her car was parked in its usual spot. Cursing under his breath, he spun his Yukon around and gunned it towards Taylour's place.

As he drove up the driveway to her house, he slowed down so as to observe where her property started. He stopped the car, got out, and felt the wind blowing softly from the north. He was approaching her house from the south. He observed the ground and found that the rain from the previous day had turned the top few inches of dirt into mud, which meant that he would leave a trail with his Yukon, so he got back in and pulled over into the grass behind a huge sycamore tree. He opened the back of the Yukon and pulled out the two full gas containers and grunted as he placed them on the ground.

Except for the tree line about 100 feet from the house, the west side of the property was mostly tall prairie bunch grass, so Roman was able to traverse the field without being seen from the road. The containers were heavy, but Roman managed to carry them without too much effort. Beads of sweat started to roll down his face as he trekked in a tight circle for a quarter of a mile. His intent was to walk parallel to the house and approach it from the north, so he turned right at the bottom of the gulley and followed the contour of the hill. After several minutes of walking his muscles started to ache from the strain, so he stopped for a few moments to rest.

The vegetation had started to get a little thicker, with less grass but more shrub oaks dotting the hillside. He could barely make out a small worn path that continued around to the right out of sight, which most likely led up to the house, so he looked for a good spot just below the path.

Roman couldn't believe his luck as he found exactly what he needed, a burnt tree that had been struck by lightning the night before.

The bolt of lightning had hit the black walnut tree straight through the heart of the trunk, effectively splitting it almost in half. The area at the base of the tree was charred from the heat of the blast, but any fire had been effectively snuffed out quickly by the rain.

Roman made his way to the tree and looked up the hill towards the house. The wind was still blowing lightly from the north and had not shifted at all, so he opened one of the gas containers and proceeded to douse the grass and shrubs with the flammable liquid. He worked his way up the side of the hill so as to direct the flames towards the unsuspecting structures found at the top. With one can empty, he continued dumping a rough cone shape that spread out from the tree.

The pungent odor of the fumes was all around him, so he quickly went back to the stricken tree and pulled out his lighter. Just as he was about to light the flame, he heard a truck driving on the road to his left and behind him. Instinctively, he ducked down out of sight and watched a black Ford F350 slowly pass by. As soon as it was out of sight, he jumped back up and brushed himself off. He sniffed and turned his head at the smell. He had accidentally landed in a patch of grass that he had just doused with the gasoline, so he tore off his shirt, wadded it up into a ball, and tossed it aside to retrieve later.

Even though there had been rain the night before, a good half an inch in spots, the moisture had already soaked through the parched landscape. Roman didn't expect too much smoldering, but that was exactly what he got when he flicked his lighter. The thirsty flame flared up at first, but without a continuous path to the next area of fumes, the fire quickly went out.

Roman went from one spot to the next, trying to light the hillside up, but soon realized that he was not going to be successful without some help from Mother Nature, who was not so inclined to accommodate.

However, just when Roman believed that the fire would not start, a spark from his lighter hit just the right spot, which turned into a flame, then a self-sustained fire, and then a blaze that quickly grew and advanced towards Taylour's home. The wind, still coming from the north, was now pushing the wildfire in the direction of Dixxon Manor. Every minute that passed, the inferno consumed the grass, shrubs, and even trees in its path.

The Fallen Body

But Roman didn't wait to watch the destruction. He gathered his containers up and ran back to his parked Yukon without looking back. Only after he had put the containers away and jumped back into his vehicle did he stare at the smoke billowing up from the tops of the trees. He smiled and turned the car around, beating a hasty retreat.

Chapter 42

George Frockmeier, Taylour's neighbor who lived about a mile down the road, was outside replacing the hay in his barn. As he emerged from the sweaty work to get something to drink from his farmhouse, he noticed the smoke coming from the direction of Dixxon Manor. Because his view in that direction was partially blocked by the tall sycamore trees that bordered his property with that of his neighbor to the west, he scrambled up the stairs to the second floor window in his bedroom. He squinted his eyes as he peered through the distorted glass, and what he saw was unmistakable. There was a prairie fire in the distance, no doubt about it.

Mr. Frockmeier stumbled over to the other side of the bed, where he grabbed the phone and dialed 9-1-1. After reporting the fire to the dispatcher at the other end, he hustled down the stairs and ran towards the hose that he was situated in the northwest corner of his property. George didn't think that the blaze would come in their direction because of how the wind was blowing, but he didn't want to take any chances as things could change quickly in a prairie wildfire.

The Fallen Body

"Barbara, we have a problem!" he called out for his wife, who was downstairs in her sewing room. When she emerged from the front door and onto their porch, she yelled, "George, what's wrong?" She walked down the steps and followed the vanishing figure of her husband around the side of the clapboard house, which had stood there for over 100 years. As she approached George from behind, she could see the rising smoke coming from the distance.

"Oh, my!" she gasped. George, seeing her now, motioned for her to help him pull the hose out as far as it would stretch. When he reached the limits of the 200 foot water hose, she turned the faucet on full blast and then hustled down the slope of the hill and over to where George was standing. He was dousing the yard with as much as was possible. She grabbed the end and told him that he needed to go over to Dixxon Manor as Taylour was sure to be at work.

"Do you have this under control?" he asked. When she nodded, he scrambled back up the hill, fired up the old Chevy truck, and sputtered his way along the dirt road that connected their properties.

When he arrived in front of the house, he could see the flames licking at the trees and sparks flying towards him. He located the hose, turned it on full blast, and proceeded down the slight drop to soak as much of the land between the house and the fire as he could.

As luck would have it, the wind had shifted coming from the north to coming from the south, pushing the flames away from the house. As the fire turned back on itself, the lack of new fuel to feed it finally choked it off. The smoke from the burnt grass hung in the air before catching the breeze. The ground was hot where George was standing, but at least the inferno had died down and no more flames were visible. Just as quickly as it had started, it smoldered and went out.

George kept spraying the slope for good measure until he was satisfied that it would not start up again spontaneously. He wiped the sweat from his brow as he gathered up the hose and started to put it back where it had been before.

He heard the wail of the fire truck siren before he saw the source of the sound. The red engine with its lights flashing made its way to the driveway and stopped near the fire hydrant. Three firefighters spilled out of the back seat and quickly went to work. One went to ready the valve on the hydrant while two others pulled on the hose so that it could be attached. They worked quickly and efficiently, even though the fire was mostly out. George retreated so as not to be in the way as they worked.

Just then, Taylour pulled up in her car. She leapt out and rushed over to George, who had just finished winding up the hose.

"George, what happened?" she asked incredulously.

"Taylour, everything is OK. It was just a small grass fire." As he turned back to look at the blackened earth, it suddenly hit him how close Taylour had come to losing her house to the flames.

"I can't believe this happened! George, do you know what caused it?"

"I have no idea, but it looks like it got put out just in time from the looks of it." George frowned and shook his head. "Unless last night's lightning storm cause a spark that suddenly flared up now, I suspect that it could have been caused by a motorist throwing his cigarette butt out the window." He raised his hand toward the road, which was barely visible through the smoke.

The Fallen Body

Despite how dirty George looked, with his blackened face and soot-covered shirt, Taylour gave him a huge hug. "Thanks for helping out, George. I owe you one!"

Embarrassed by her spontaneous show of affection, George's face reddened. "Aw, it was nothin'. That's what neighbors are for. To look out for one another." They both winced at the smell of smoke that wafted towards them.

"Well, if it hadn't been for your quick thinking, I'm sure that my house would have burned to the ground. Really, I am quite thankful to you." Taylour patted him on the shoulder as they turned to go back to George's Chevy truck. She waved at him as he drove off.

Chapter 43

Roman started sweating and wiping his brow with his sleeve as he listened to the latest tape recording from Taylour's law office. Every effort to slow down or scare her off of the Baines murder investigation was having the opposite effect.

"…I need to speak with Mr. Philip Davidson, please." Taylour's voice sounded a bit hollow, but otherwise it was if she was standing in the same room as Roman.

"He's not here right now. Can I please take a message?" came the reply from the receptionist. The other end sounded further away and not as clear, so Roman turned the volume up slightly.

"Does he have voicemail?"

"Yes, he does. One moment, please."

A series of clicks and silence followed, and then Philip's strong and confident pre-recorded message was heard.

"…please leave a message after the tone." Beep.

"Hi, Philip, this is Taylour." Roman winced at the familiarity of her tone, and then wiped his brow again. "I need to talk to you about, er, what happened earlier today. The latest going on around here. I'm really beginning to think that someone is deliberately trying to scare me off this case, and I have no idea who that might be."

Roman smiled and sat back. He hadn't been discovered. What a relief! But that feeling was short-lived as the next part of the message sent a chill of fear through him.

"…can't help but think that someone is watching me." Pause, and then a deep exhale of air from Taylour. "I've seen a stranger in town. He's a foreign-looking…" She struggled to find the right words. "…dude, all scary looking, and I honestly thought that he wanted to hurt me when I glanced behind me in the produce aisle at the store yesterday, and I thought he might have been following me, so I went towards him, but he vanished and I don't know where he went."

Another sigh, and then, "Sorry, don't mean to… er… ramble on. I tried calling your cell phone, but it didn't pick up, so there may have been a problem with the signal going through. Sometimes the coverage here in beautiful Marlinsville… er… ah… isn't so good. But you don't need to know that, or care… so call me when you can." The distinct clunk of the headset marked the end of the call.

* * *

Roman's gaze followed Sarah as she pulled out the gun and dropped it in the trash can. She then disappeared into the shadows.

He slowly got out of his vehicle, put a pair of leather gloves on, and then glanced around as he walked towards the trash. Seeing no one, he reached his hand in and fished out the gun. He placed it gently into his overcoat pocket, pulled his Fedora over his eyes and furtively made his way towards the entrance of The Residence.

The Fallen Body

Waiting for just the right moment, he slid in behind an elderly lady who had rung for the doorman, had woken him up, and was now occupying his attention with tales of Snookie and how he wasn't feeling well. He rounded the corner without being seen and headed towards the stairs. He swung the stair door opened and proceeded to jog up the twenty flights to his destination.

Having reached the 20th floor, he paused to catch his breath. Once he was able to breathe normally, he tiptoed to number 2001. He paused to listen to any activity on the other side of the door, and when he heard none, he brandished Sarah's .22 and knocked on the door.

When the door opened, he forced his way in, pushing Neal back with his left hand in front of him. Neal had a cell phone up to his ear and nearly dropped it as he scrambled backwards.

"Where is she?" the mystery man asked.

"Where's who?"

"You know who I mean. Where is your client?"

"Uh, you're going to have to be more specific than that."

"Quit playing games with me!" He stepped forward with the gun pointed squarely at Mr. Baines' chest and pulled the trigger, twice.

Bam! Bam!

Neal's body fell backwards from the impact. He was dead before he hit the ground, the cell phone falling to the carpet.

The shooter placed the gun back into his jacket, picked up the cell phone and clicked it closed. He grabbed Neal under the arms and dragged him to the balcony. He glanced over the side, and then lifted the dead body over his head. He tossed the body away from the building, and then watched it fall, down, down. It landed like a boulder on the roof of a gray Chevrolet Impala.

He turned from the balcony and quickly took the gun out of his overcoat, carefully placing it on the ground where he had shot Neal. He surveyed the room, making sure that he did not leave any blood smears or footprints, and then exited. He flew down the stairs

The Fallen Body

to the 8th floor, opened the door, and then walked briskly to the elevator. He rode it down to the lobby, glanced left and right, and then slid out the back door to the parking lot opposite the front of the building. He heard the wailing of sirens in the distant as he slinked into the night. He would come back for his car tomorrow.

* * *

Roman sat back, slowly rubbed his mouth and his chin with his hand, and then stared at the wall. He needed to escalate his efforts before Taylour discovered the truth.

Chapter 44

The package arrived in Friday's mail along with the electric bill and the rent invoice that was marked "Past Due." It was tucked in between the most recent court papers for the Johnson vs. Johnson case and the title paperwork from last week's Robinson escrow home closing. The envelope was non-descriptive and plain, but a stamp of "Sensitive Materials Enclosed" was placed on the bottom left of both the front and back. The postmark was faint -- only the "eton, NJ" was discernible -- and the rest was smeared from what appeared to be a gray, dirty shoe print. The corners were mashed in and crumpled, but the address had been handwritten precisely by the sender, Pierre Fontanot.

Dave, the postal worker, came into the office, looked around for Spencer, and when he didn't see him, dropped the bundle on Spencer's desk and took the outgoing mail that was already in the familiar shelf marked "Outgoing." He turned to go, the entrance bell announcing his departure almost as an afterthought. A chill hung in the air from the brief exposure to the frosty outside.

The Fallen Body

The wall clock ticked softly, and the sound of a car passing by filtered through the big pane windows. The closed window slats rustled against each other as a slight breeze passed through the heater vent, trying its best to warm up the front office. The distant, muffled sound of music playing through ear buds grew louder as Spencer returned to the front with an empty box. Humming and bouncing slightly to the beat, Spencer pushed aside today's mail and placed the box squarely on his desk. With his eyes half closed, he proceeded to take the files from the bottom filing cabinet and place them in the box. He moved quickly while simultaneously filling up the cardboard container and keeping the headphones plugged securely into his ears.

As he lifted up the box to take it to the back for archiving, he inadvertently knocked that day's mail bundle off of the desk. It fell with a light thump and somehow wedged itself behind the artificial tree and the wall, out of view. Spencer, gyrating even more from the tunes emanating from his iPod, did not see the mail fall as he turned and walked back down the hall.

* * *

On that same crisp December morning, with the frost receding as the sun came out, Taylour was half on, half off her couch. She had a worn afghan pulled up to her chin, but the haphazard way in which it covered her indicated that Taylour had not slept well.

Indeed, she had not slept well at all. Tossing and turning all night long, she finally drifted off in front of the TV at around 3 a.m. while watching Carrie Smith on the Home Shopping Network. After she fell asleep, she dreamed about an endless pile of briefs stacking up all around her, and then she faintly heard a phone. The sound grew louder and louder, causing her head to throb.

Startled out of her dream, she woke up to the same ringing coming from the phone in the kitchen.

Bleary-eyed, she fumbled with the remote to turn the TV off, and then stumbled to answer the metallic clanging that was attached to the wall in the kitchen. However, when she put the receiver to her ear, all she heard was a dial tone. Mumbling to herself, she glanced at the digital clock. When she saw the numbers change from 9:15 change to 9:16, she immediately rushed to the bathroom to take a quick shower. It took longer than she wanted, but she managed to get dressed, pull her wet mop of hair back into a ponytail, and launch herself through the front door in under 15 minutes.

When she arrived at her office, Taylour plopped her bag onto her desk and went to see what Spencer was doing. She found him in the back room stacking boxes of old files.

"Spencer!" Nothing. It was then that she heard the heavy metal gyrations of "Hats Off to the Bull" by Chevelle coming from Spencer's ear buds.

"Spencer!" She still got no response, so Taylour poked him hard on the shoulder.

"Oh, hey, have you been there long?"

"I've been shouting your name. No wonder you can't hear me, you have your music cranked up. You're gonna go deaf, y'know."

"What?"

Taylour playfully punched him on the arm and asked, "Sorry I'm late this morning. Why didn't you wake me this morning so that we could come in to work together?"

"Sorry, but you looked like you needed your rest and all. I wanted to come in early and organize your files by putting some of your older case files here in the back. I hope that's OK?"

Taylour gave him a slight grin. He really was trying hard. "I appreciate your help, I really do."

"It's just been, well, hard to get my mind off of Dog." Spencer's eyes got moist. "What happened to him, Taylour?"

She shook her head. "I have no idea, but I don't think that it was a random act. Someone is warning us off, and with his death…" She stopped to take a breath. "That, and the fire near our house, it all has the markings of someone trying very hard to rattle me."

"Why? Who'd want to harm you? You're, like, the nicest person I know. Taking me in and all, with no advanced warning, after showing up at your doorstep. That takes, well, guts to do something like that."

Taylour laughed at the concerned look on Spencer's face. His sincerity, along with his adoration for her, made her heart swell. She wrapped her arms around him and gave him a tight squeeze. "My protector!"

She sensed a bit of awkwardness as Spencer slowly brought his arms up to hug her back, and then suddenly she felt the crushing of his grip as he gave into his emotions and sobbed. His entire body shook with pain as he held her like a vice. Finally, he pulled away from her and held her at arm's length.

"Sorry 'bout that. Don't know what came over me." He sniffed softly and wiped his nose with his sleeve.

Taylour bit her lower lip and cast her gaze downward as they separated. She cleared her throat and told him that everything would be alright. She sauntered back to her private office and sat down in her chair. She stared for a time at the ceiling, running question after question over in her mind. The food poisoning at the restaurant, the brutal killing of Dog, and now a fire that almost burned down her home. They can't all be coincidences, can they?

Suddenly she sat up straight. *I know how I can find out who might be doing this!*

She grabbed her coat and keys and headed for the door. She yelled over her shoulder that she was going out, and then she whisked down the hall. Just as Taylour was about to push open the door, she whirled around as something out of place caught her eye.

She moved Spencer's chair out of the way and bent down to get the mail that had fallen previously. She pushed the tree aside and sneezed from the small dust cloud that arose, and then stretched her arm and fingers until she came into contact with the bundle. She felt a slight twinge in her left shoulder as her fingers wrapped around the item. She placed the package on the desk and started to go through it.

"Hey, it looks like Dave has been by with the mail," Spencer said as he ambled up to the desk.

Taylour was about to ask why the mail had been haphazardly dropped from view, but she bit her tongue and said nothing. She picked up the envelope from Pierre, and once she realized who it was from, she tore it open, spilling the contents onto the desk.

Her heart skipped a beat when she saw the personal note from Pierre, which stated that he would make himself available to talk to her if she had any questions. "Oh, Pierre. I'm so sorry!" She wiped the tear from her eye and took a deep breath before diving into the contents.

She cleared a space on Spencer's desk and excitedly glanced through the newspaper clippings, flipping them over quickly once she had the chance to glean the details

The Fallen Body

from the article. They all mentioned a Dmitri Polzin, who was being charged with racketeering under the RICO statutes in a federal court somewhere in New York. One of the articles included a photo of Dmitri, whose hard stare back at Taylour sent a tiny shiver of fear up her spine.

Next came the photos, and Taylour's face blanched as she saw the gruesome details. A dead body in an awkward pose. Bruises on the face. Blood pooled under the neck and head. Taylour turned the pictures over and took several deep breaths to calm herself. She wasn't prepared for what came next.

After Taylour flipped to the last photo, she gasped at the face that was staring up at her. A small rustling pierced the silence as the photos fell from her fingers.

She tried to force down the wave of nausea that passed over her as she staggered to the bathroom.

"Hey, Taylour, where do you want th-- Whoa! You don't look too good."

Taylour stumbled into the bathroom and went straight to the sink, where she splashed water on her face. Her body shook silently as the fear gripped her. She tried to compose herself by taking long, deep intakes of air and closing her eyes, but all she could imagine was herself in the same pose as the dead victim.

"Taylour!" She seemed to snap out of her horror show when she heard her name coming from just outside the door. She saw Spencer shuffling his feet, still in the hall, not knowing exactly what to do, but then Philip burst passed him and cradled her face in his hands.

Taylour let all of her emotions out. She grabbed Philip and cried. Her body shook as her salty tears ran down her face. Philip talked softly in her ear, telling

Taylour that she was OK, that nothing was going to happen to her, and she eventually stopped her sobbing.

She let go of Philip and began to wipe her face with her hand. "Ah, s-sorry about that," she said.

"I saw the photos on the desk," Philip said as he reached for a tissue. He handed it to her, and she cracked a smile up at him.

"That's him!"

Philip tipped his head sideways and scrunched his eyes. "Who?"

"The man in the photo, wearing a dark suit. That's him! That's who's been following me around."

"You mean the foreign-looking guy that you described in your voicemail? He's here?"

"Yes! Who is he?

"I dunno. I can run it past a few people. Are you sure it's him?

Taylour nodded. After wiping her eyes and nose, she said, "I-I'm sure I look like a-a mess!"

"You look beautiful! You're just a little scared from what you just saw."

Her hands went to her hair as a flush came across her face. "You're sweet to say that." She tossed the tissue away and turned to look at herself in the mirror and groaned inwardly at her reflection.

"Look, Taylour, those pictures were not of you."

Her lips and chin began to tremble, so she took a deep breath. "No, they weren't of me, but that will be my fate if we don't figure out what is going on with this case!"

Philip shook his head. "No, that is *not* your fate. I won't let anything happen to you."

His intensity surprised her. She gazed into Philips eyes and saw both strength and concern. She was

The Fallen Body

uncomfortable at this sudden escalation of their relationship, so she cleared her throat and lightly placed her hand on his chest in an effort to move past him.

He grabbed her by the wrist, looked down at her eyes, and then kissed her. She resisted for about a half of a second, and then all of her reserve melted away as she felt the urgency of his embrace. Philip let go of her wrist and grabbed her by the nape of her neck and pulled her closer. She lightly caressed his face with her hand.

The sweetness of emotions that washed over her caused Taylour to forget her troubles, even if it was only for a brief moment. However, reality has a way of settling, hard, and this was no exception.

She pulled away slightly, and then averted her gaze downward. "I-I don't know what came over me." She adjusted her hair again, but couldn't muster the courage to look at Philip. "I-I gotta go, er, uh…"

She pushed past him and left him standing there, a stunned look on his face. He didn't rush after her as his feet seemed frozen to the ground, unable to move. Finally, he ran his hand through his gray hair, lightly touching his scar, and then he turned to leave, his feet a bit unsteady.

Spencer was witness to all of this, but Philip didn't acknowledge him as he brushed past. Taylour was standing in the front of the office, supporting herself with her left hand on the desk, her face downcast. Philip reached the door, hesitated, and then pushed it open slowly. The bell on the door pierced the silence with its high tinny sound, and then he was gone. The smell of his Burberry cologne hung in the air.

Taylour couldn't hold back the smile as it crept over her face. She felt like a teenager, as if she was experiencing her first crush over again, and she liked how it made her feel.

Chapter 45

Roman needed some air, so he decided to take a walk. As he headed towards the downtown area, he saw that the town had decorated for their annual Christmas festival and had invited various vendors to participate, which they did willingly and regularly. Temporary booths with white canvas tops all in a row were set up along Pine Avenue, which ran perpendicular to Main Street just one block over from the county courthouse. The majestic stone building was adorned with green, white, and red balloons to celebrate the Christmas season.

The crowd of people grew larger as the steady stream of cars and trucks disgorged their occupants, while shouts of "Merry Christmas" and "Happy Holidays" mingled with the imploring of small children to have their turn with Santa Claus. However, as each one spotted the portly fellow dressed in red silk and white cotton and black boots, they would suddenly turn shy and hide behind their parents' legs. Some even cried – perhaps it was the inability to clearly see his face obscured by unnaturally curly locks that scratched their cheeks when placed on Old Saint Nick's lap – while "Aahs" and "Oohs" came from parents and grandparents as they

The Fallen Body

snapped photo after photo of this terrifying, wonderful rite of the season.

The aroma of cinnamon buns and churros and funnel cake wafted over the revelers as they stopped and gazed through the windows of the different stores, such as Misty's Mistletoe Shoppe or Gadgets 'n Gizmos or Trains R Us. Packages bumped against each other when going in opposite directions, while their carriers bundled up in their mittens and festive sweaters given to them from distant relations.

Someone thrust a flier at him, so he grabbed it and read it with an annoyed frown. It was about the sweater contest and when the judging would commence. According to the flier, there were prizes given out for the ugliest, hideous and scratchiest garments. Bragging rights for the winners would last the entire year.

As Roman took in the scene before him, wandering up and down the street, it didn't occur to him that he might run into someone that he knew, someone that he didn't want to know that he was there.

It occurred by the huge Christmas tree that was adorned earlier in the month and sat in the plaza just south of a small playground full of swinging and spinning children. The evergreen stood over thirty feet tall and was almost ten feet in diameter. Candy canes, ribbons, glitter, gold and silver ball ornaments, and colored lights had been placed carefully to cover all bare spots. The tree gave the impression of fragility, but it was quite stable as the stand it sat in was bolted securely into the concrete.

Roman was reminded of the Christmas tree in Rockefeller Center in New York and thought this one to be a poor imitation. As he turned to go, he accidentally bumped into a strawberry blonde woman taking a picture of a younger man dressed in reindeer antlers and a sweater that was the ugliest thing that he had ever seen. When he recognized Taylour as the person he had bumped into, he mumbled his apologies and stalked away.

* * *

Taylour stood there, puzzled. *Where have I seen him before?* She ran his face through her mind, and then suddenly went pale. He was the same man that I saw in the pictures sent by Pierre! She jerked around to see if she could still see him, and she spotted his towering frame as he hustled away, about seventy feet away.

She put her camera away and motioned for Spencer to follow her.

"What is it, Taylour?" Spencer asked.

"I, uh, think I just saw someone."

"Who?"

Taylour quickened her pace, and said nothing. Spencer had to half jog to keep up.

She was within twenty feet of the bulking figure when he turned around. He saw that Taylour was in hot pursuit, so he turned abruptly down a side alley. Taylour noticed his clenched jaw and what she thought was fear on his face.

Without any thought of her safety, she ran to where he had turned and came to a sudden stop. She stood up on her toes and peered over the heads of the crowd. When she spotted him duck into a doorway and disappear, she resumed her chase.

Spencer followed right behind her, his antlers falling to the ground. He didn't have time to scoop them up before they were stomped on by the swarm of people on the sidewalk.

As Taylour approached the door, the smell of caramel apples and cotton candy assaulted her, which reminded her of the Six Flags amusement park. It was such a pleasant aroma that she almost forgot what she was doing. She shook her head to clear it, and then pushed her way in.

The aisles were packed with shoppers as they chatted noisily with each other, but she was able to see her target as he pushed his way forcefully to the back room and out the back door. She apologized to those that were in her way, saying "Excuse me" when she could, but her progress through the store was brought almost to a standstill.

When she finally entered the back room, she heard someone yell at her that she shouldn't be back here, but Taylour remained undeterred. As she pushed her way through the poorly lit area, she accidentally knocked over an opened box of hard candy, which came crashing down behind her. She glanced behind her and saw Spencer dodge the fallen sweets, which had scattered to every spare corner of the dingy space, and then he was by her side.

"Taylour, who are we chasing?" Just then, a large African American woman, fifty years old with a no-nonsense look on her face arrived, her one hand on her hip and the other pointing at Taylour accusingly.

"You're gonna have to pay for that, y' know."

Taylour fought her impulse to leave and continue her pursuit, but thought better of it.

"I'm sorry about that. I'll be happy to pay for any damages that may have been incurred." Taylour reached for her wallet and pulled out a five-dollar bill and handed it over.

"Ha, that ain't nearly enough to pay for all the damages that you caused, not t' mention the mess that you made." She swept her arm towards the front of the store, where several display cases had been knocked over, their contents askew or knocked over. Taylour slumped her shoulders and shuffled back into the bright glare of the retail shop.

After offering to clean up the mess and being handed a broom without comment, Taylour started sweeping up the chunks of candy. The place looked like it hadn't been mopped in a while, but Taylour felt bad about what had transpired and considered any extra effort on her part to be her penance. She even spent a few moments organizing the boxes of chocolates and toffees and bonbons that she found, stacking them up by type, thus creating a better pathway through the inventory.

At long last, Taylour glanced through the open door to the front of the store and noticed that Spencer had already righted the display cases and was now chatting with the same woman in between customers. She called herself Honey Vender, and her booming voice was unmistakable. Taylour watched Spencer's animated retelling of the pursuit and smiled when she heard Honey laugh.

When she was finally done with her work, Taylour apologized again to Honey for the mess that they had made. She turned out to be the owner of the candy store, and invited them back real soon.

"But only if you promise not to make another mess, y' hear?" Wagging her finger at them again, playfully this time, Honey let out a belly laugh at the two of them as they retreated from the store, and then went back to her patrons.

Once they were clear of the noise from the revelers, Spencer grabbed Taylour by the elbow and asked, "Are you gonna tell me what's goin' on, Auntie?"

The Fallen Body

Taylour pursed her lips. "Spencer, we have a problem that needs fixing. It's time we had a little heart-to-heart conversation with the sheriff."

Chapter 46

A hidden figure lay sleeping in a king sized bed with a comforter pulled up to an unshaven chin. A light wheezing could be heard from the bed's occupant, and the lumpiness of the bed rose up and down in concert with the snoring.

The stillness was suddenly interrupted by a harsh ringing that came from a decades-old wall phone. A sharp, abrupt snort from the bed, and then the figure bolted from the covers. Muttering under his breath, Sheriff Lyman Grayson reached for the source of the buzzing that had interrupted his slumber.

"This better be good."

He listened to the voice on the other end, holding the phone in one hand, while rubbing his eyes as if to push the dreariness away.

The room was just big enough to hold a nightstand and a five-drawer dresser, which had been purchased from the nearby Wal-Mart many years ago. The laminate boards had lost their shape and form long ago, and the nightstand was unremarkable except for the orange lava lamp and digital clock that rested on it under a thin layer of dust.

The Fallen Body

"Ms. Dixxon, do you know what time it is?" he barked into the receiver. "Dad gummit, I barely got any sleep on account of all the folks coming from miles around for last night's festival" – he pronounced it fes-tee-val – "and we've been short-handed ever since Percy fell off his horse. I--"

Taylour's next words froze him in his tracks and all sleepiness vanished.

"Where you at, your office?" he said, a little less abrasively this time. More sounds coming from Taylour, and then Sheriff Grayson responded. "Give me thirty minutes to get freshened up, then I'll meet you there." After getting an affirmative on the other end, he hung up without saying goodbye.

The 62 year-old went into action. He took a quick shower, got dressed in his brown uniform, strapped on his holster, straightened the chocolate tie that hung tightly around his neck, smoothed off some imaginary lint from his beige, dual pocketed, buttoned shirt, and then checked the time on his nightstand.

More mutterings about not getting any fresh coffee, and then he rushed out the door. He ambled to his patrol car and huffed as he slid into his seat. He turned on the flashing neon lights and accelerated straight out of his driveway and onto the main thoroughfare.

As he breezed past the courthouse, he glanced at the city workers who were taking down the vendor booths. The city had decided to leave the Christmas tree in place, so it stood out, all alone, in the plaza.

There was very little traffic at this time of the morning, so Sheriff Grayson made the trip to Taylour's office in record time. He pulled his vehicle into the designated handicap parking spot and sauntered up to the front door. He put his head to the window to peer in, shading his eyes so that he could see the interior of the office, and saw Spencer staring back at him.

Taylour wormed her way past Spencer and opened the door for the sheriff. He greeted her with a nod and a curt "Morning," and then let her lead him back to her private office. Spencer followed closely behind and pulled the ear buds from his ears.

"Sheriff, we have a problem. We—"

"Before, when you said there's a killer on the loose downtown, how serious were you? If y' said that to get my attention, y' got it."

"Sheriff, I understand that you may have some misgivings about—"

"Ms. Dixxon, I do *not* have issues with you and your kind. Quite the contrary, I thought very highly of your father as a respected member of this community." He set his jaw into a hard smile. "But this nonsense about a killer loose in the community, that doesn't set well with me."

"If you would simply hear me out, I—"

"I have heard you, Ms. Dixxon, and frankly, I'm tired of the implications that we are not doing our job, that somehow we missed seeing a murderer in our midst."

"I have not made any such implications, I simply want to—"

"Then why have you had me investigate the fire at your farm that was obviously caused by a lightning strike, or your mutt who clearly broke its neck in an unfortunate fall, or simply a bad case of food poisoning?" He crossed his arms. "And now you are saying that we have not been able to catch this so-called criminal, who is now walking among us, endangering our women and children." He shook his head. "That doesn't set well at all, Ms. Dixxon."

The Fallen Body

Taylour slammed both hands on her desk, which made everyone jump. She leaned into the sheriff.

"Lyman Theodore Grayson! I am *not* implying any such thing, nor have I *ever* said anything that would give you any reason to believe that, I swear on my dead parents' grave!"

"Now, you listen here, young lady, I—"

"No, *Sheriff*, you listen here. The man that Spencer and I saw yesterday is the same man in this picture." She picked up from her desk and held up the same photo of Roman that she had received from Pierre. "This man has been linked to these murders." She grabbed the photos of the dead bodies and thrust them out to the sheriff.

Startled from her sudden outburst, he took the photos slowly, and then raised his eyebrows at what he saw. Frowning, he started to open his mouth, but then closed it. He rubbed his chin, and then finally spoke.

"Never seen him before." He sat back with a wry smile on his face. "And he seems to be the type that you wouldn't miss in a crowd, right?"

He turned to Spencer. "Did you see him too?"

"I, uh, didn't get a good look at him, sir."

The sheriff turned back to Taylour. "So, how far away were you when you saw his face?"

Taylour backed into her chair, turned her head, and mumbled, "Well, he almost bumped into me."

Sensing an opening, he pushed further. "But did you get a good look at him?"

"Er, no. Not until he turned back and saw us coming after him."

"And how far away were you then?"

Taylour paused and let out a sigh. "About twenty feet or so."

The Fallen Body

He pulled himself out of his chair and stood in the center of the room. "And this was at what time of the day?"

Taylour dropped her head and put her hand to her forehead. "Look, I know where this is going. Did I get a good look at him, well enough to know the color of his eyes? No, I didn't. But—"

"But nothin', Ms. Dixxon. Y' didn't get a good look at him, and neither did Spencer, so what do I have to go on?" He got up from his seat.

Taylour slumped into her chair again.

The sheriff turned to go, so Taylour got up from her chair to follow him out. When they passed the kitchen, they both got a whiff of the tuna sandwiches that Spencer had made for his lunch.

"Sheriff, wait! I just remembered something that might be a clue." She ran down the hallway to catch up with him. "When he bumped into me, I recall the smell of fish or tuna. It was very distinct."

"Is that all, Ms. Dixxon?"

"Look, I know it's not much, but at least it's something…" Her voice trailed off as he pushed his way out the door without saying another word.

Spencer, who was right behind her, said, "Sorry, Taylour, I guess I should have looked harder at him."

"That's OK, don't blame yourself."

"The sheriff really has it in for you."

"The sheriff's a good man, just a bit ornery. Nothing I can't handle."

Taylour put her hand on Spencer's shoulder, looked him straight in the eye, and said, "Hang in there, Spencer. We need to keep our wits about us as this man, whoever he is, is extremely dangerous. I don't want anything to happen to either of us, so be careful."

The Fallen Body

"I will, Taylour, I will."

Chapter 47

Sheriff Grayson had a favorite spot just out of town where he liked to catch people exceeding the speed limit, both coming and going. Most locals were familiar with this speed trap, so the drivers that he clocked going too fast were almost always out-of-towners passing through. It was a lucrative business for the city, so Sheriff Grayson made it a point to spend a few hours of his eight hour shift there.

After he picked up two grilled chicken sandwiches and some freshly squeezed lemonade at the Chick-Fil-A, he positioned his squad car on the west side of the north/southbound road and faced south towards Marlinsville. The road, called Farm-to-Market, or FM 69, allowed him to park behind a faded billboard for a Dairy Queen long since gone. It sat directly on the ground, thus it obscured the view of those coming down the hill as they arrived into town. It was also right where the speed limit dropped from 65 mph to 55, and then to 45 mph, so he had that working for him as well.

He pointed his radar gun directly through the windshield and waited. Last month he finally was able to convince the town council that he needed a video camera, which sat next to the radar gun and ran on a continuous loop. It recorded all traffic stops that he made, and it was used as visual evidence in traffic court as needed.

After about five minutes, his first speeder passed by going 75 mph in a 45 mph, so he quickly started up the car, flicked his lights on, and burst onto the road in record time. He floored the accelerator and caught up with the car in record time. It was the latest Chevy Camaro, flaming red, and the sheriff almost felt sorry for having pulled it over because it was such a sweet car.

He knocked on the window and indicated to the driver to roll it down. He calmly explained to the 25 year old blonde how fast she had been going and asked for her driver's license and registration. She pulled her registration from the glove compartment, and her hands shook as she fumbled in her giant purse for her ID. She turned her blue, tear-stained eyes up at the sheriff, hoping to catch a break of some kind, but he was undeterred. He had heard every excuse in the book in his thirty years on the force, and rarely did he have even the slightest bit of compassion for those that he pulled over.

As he was writing the ticket, she smiled up at him and tried placing her soft, warm hand on his arm, but when she saw him lower his head and give her a hard, cold stare, she pulled it back as if she had touched a hot stove. Her nostrils flared as she grabbed the ticket from him, put her car into gear, and headed on to her destination, slower this time.

Sheriff Grayson chuckled to himself as he sauntered back to his squad car. *This day might not turn out to be too bad after all.* He squeezed himself back into his vehicle and repositioned it back where he had been before.

The sheriff turned on the radio and picked up a station from Waco that was playing Christmas songs, so he left it there. He was humming to one of his favorites, "Grandma Got Run Over By A Reindeer," when he caught another speeder on his radar. He turned the car on again, flicked his lights on one more time, and shot out from his hiding place. As he approached the vehicle from behind, the song finished, so the sheriff went to turn it off, but his hand never made it to the dial.

The driver appeared to be ignoring him, so Sheriff Grayson decided to turn on his siren to get his attention. Finally, after about two minutes of tailing the vehicle, it decided to pull over.

The vehicle was a black GMC Yukon.

Chapter 48

John Barker was going to be late for work, and he was frantic. He couldn't afford to be late again. His boss had warned him that if he clocked in even one minute after the start of his shift, "There would be consequences." John couldn't stand his boss, but this was the only job around, so he didn't have much of a choice.

As he sped out of town, he saw the sheriff's squad car parked on the other side of the road, but at an odd angle. Cursing under his breath, he slowed his truck down and said a little prayer that he would not get pulled over. As he got closer, he noticed an odd, brown shape just in front and off to the side of the police cruiser. When he passed by, he swore out loud as he saw that it was a body sprawled out on the edge of the pavement.

Without thinking, John slammed on his brakes, put his truck into park and jumped out. He ran over and knelt down next to the sheriff, and then turned him onto his back. He saw two bullet holes through the crimson stain on the sheriff's uniform. John's hand shook as he felt for a pulse, which was thready and weak. He glanced around and tried to see if anyone had stopped or seen what had just transpired. Just as he was about to call 9-1-1 from his

The Fallen Body

cell phone, John heard a garbage truck lift up a dumpster and drop it back down on the solid concrete with a loud bang. He yelled and waved his arms to get the driver's attention, but the truck moved off down the street without noticing the scene. He debated leaving the sheriff there all by himself, and then realized that he still had his phone.

John frantically pounded out the numbers to the emergency dispatcher, getting blood on the phone. The phone rang and rang with no answer.

"C'mon, c'mon!"

Finally, a dispatcher answered the call. "Thank you for calling 911, this is Phyllis McIntyre, how may--"

"Someone shot the sheriff! He's still alive, but he needs help!"

The dispatcher took the information on where John was and promised to get someone there immediately. "I am going to stay on the phone with you until help arrives, OK?"

"Thanks."

John continued to apply pressure to the two wounds so as to minimize the bleeding. Within a minute or two he heard the far-off sound of a siren. Once the ambulance slid to a stop, kicking up loose gravel, two Emergency Medical Technicians leaped out and ran towards the sheriff and John. He stepped back as they went to work.

The siren and flashing lights attracted a small group of neighbors, like moths to a porch light. As they milled around, someone named Mackie approached John, who was still in shock, and asked him what happened. John told Mackie what he knew and the news spread like wildfire. Pretty soon there was a sizeable crowd.

The Fallen Body

Just then a deputy sheriff pulled up in his squad car, and then another. They immediately set to work to secure the sheriff's car and the rest of the crime scene, asking people to maintain a respectful distance. The adults in the crowd talked in hushed tones while their children started a game of tag on the lawn. Little Billy Jackson was being chased by his older sister Lizzie and when he let out a peal of frightened laughter, his mother shushed him and made him stand next to her, which was his punishment for not understanding the true severity of what was unfolding before them. He grabbed onto her skirt and fidgeted around her while she went back to the solemn group, who were still talking in quiet, reverent tones.

Finally, the EMT's loaded the sheriff on a gurney and wheeled him to the back of the ambulance. They drove off silently but left their lights on as they pulled out. The crowd stared as one down the road until the vehicle disappeared around the bend, and then dispersed like ghosts back to their homes.

The crime scene technicians arrived from Waco about an hour later and went to work. They secured the video from the sheriff's car, took photos of tire marks and any blood that they found, as well as any shell casings or footprints. They also interviewed John Barker extensively after taking possession of his shirt and pants, which they needed in order to eliminate any trace evidence that he might have left behind. Fortunately, the scene was roped off to prevent others from compromising the evidence.

After a few hours of work, the techs loaded up the evidence and their equipment and took it back to their lab in Waco. From there they would work hand-in-hand with the local police department to determine who committed the crime.

The Fallen Body

That night, the citizens of Marlinsville prayed for the sheriff and his recovery.

Chapter 49

Roman cursed his fortunes as he quickly gathered up his belongings. He knew that it was only a matter of time before the vehicle that he was driving would be identified by the police as being at the scene of the crime, most likely because of the video camera that was positioned to capture just those types of situations. He had watched too many episodes of "Cops" to think otherwise.

He hadn't meant to shoot the sheriff. He was furious that he had been pulled over. He had travelled that road several times and knew that the sheriff liked to pull people over from that spot. Roman had been distracted because his usual tactics of intimidation had not worked on Taylour, and after the latest escape from her at the Christmas festival, he felt vulnerable and exposed, and he didn't like that.

But the sheriff must have recognized him from somewhere, because as soon as he saw Roman' photo on his driver's license, his face went pale and he fumbled for the gun in his holster. But, because Roman already had his hand on his own gun, he was able to whip his weapon out first. He fired three quick shots at the sheriff through the open window, and then slammed his foot on the accelerator to get away. Dirt and gravel kicked up behind him, peppering the slumped body of the sheriff.

So Roman blamed what happened on bad timing. Now he had to leave town. He still had not managed to

The Fallen Body

find where Taylour had Sarah hidden, but he had one shot left. He was going to storm Taylour's home and force her to take him to where Sarah was, and then he would kill both of them.

Chapter 50

"Where you going, Taylour?" Spencer was making a grilled cheese sandwich.

"I've got some last minute Christmas shopping to do, so I am heading towards Waco."

"Nothin' like waiting until the last minute, huh?"

"Watch it, or you'll be getting coal in your stocking." Taylour chuckled. "I wanted to get something for Sarah and a few other people."

"I keep meanin' t' ask you about her. Where is she, by the way?" Spencer licked his buttery fingers after he finished dumping the two sandwiches onto a paper towel.

"For the last time, you know that I can't tell you that. You've been trying to get me to tell you since she's been in hiding."

"So, why haven't y' told me?" He made a mocking, pouty face with his lower lip.

"It's for your own good. The fewer people know where she is, the safer she will be. Especially after our most recent encounter at the festival."

"Don't you trust me?" Now Spencer was no longer being playful.

The Fallen Body

"Spencer, don't push it. I trust you as much as anyone, but I have an obligation to preserve my client's privacy. That extends to you, even though you work for me."

Taylour glanced at her watch and grabbed her keys. "I gotta go. I can't stay and discuss this with you." She grabbed a sweater jacket from the coat rack, zipped it up, and ran out the door. "Bye!"

Spencer didn't answer because he was sulking, but that didn't last long. He bit into his sandwich and said out loud, "Mm, that's good!"

He stacked the other sandwich on the first one and took his food into the family room so he could watch some college basketball. He had enjoyed the Baylor Bears beating up on Brigham Young University the night before. Now he was watching the Southern Jaguars play the Texas A&M Aggies.

He cheered as J'Mychal Reese of the Aggies broke a tie game with a jump shot to go ahead 51-49, and then he groaned when each team turned the ball over. Spencer yelled, "Miss, miss!" as Malcolm Miller of the Jaguars made two free throws to tie the game up. He was on the edge of the sofa, and then groaned when the Aggies missed a shot. He covered his eyes as Miller was fouled again with 5.8 seconds. Miller was just about to take the first of two free throws when a loud knock came from the front door.

"Who is it?" Spencer yelled. When no one answered, he backed up to the door, keeping his eyes glued to the TV, searching for the door knob with his right hand. If he hadn't been watching the game he would have peeked out of the peephole first.

The Fallen Body

Spencer groaned again when he saw Miller make the first free throw, and then he found the knob and turned it.

But instead of opening, the door stuck, so he grabbed it with both hands and pulled it, hard.

"Yeah, whadda y' want?" he said before turning to the large man on the porch.

Chapter 51

Taylour took the back way to Waco hoping to avoid traffic and was rewarded with a thirty minute delay while an accident was cleared a mile ahead of her. She finally made it to the Central Texas Marketplace off of Texas Loop 340 and found a parking spot on the outer edge of the parking lot near Newk's Cafe. She had never seen so many vehicles in the same spot since she went shopping at the last minute last Christmas the year before. *I gotta stop waiting until the last minute!*

She marched into Belk and browsed the men's wardrobe to buy a sweater for Philip, and then wandered over to the women's section. Not finding anything that jumped out at her, she paid for what she had and then left to go to Kohl's next door.

She traveled from one store to the next, carrying her purchases with her. After finding a pair of running sweats for Spencer and a 1,000 piece puzzle by Thomas Kinkade titled "Conquering the Storm" for Sarah, as well as other gifts for friends and family, she finally determined that she had bought something for everyone on her list.

As Taylour made her way to her car laden down with packages, her cell phone rang. Because her hands were full, she was unable to answer it. She finally made it to her car, put her items in the trunk, and then got in. After she started her car to warm it up, she pulled out her cell phone to see who had called. It was Philip.

She saw that he had left her three messages in the last fifteen minutes, but the messages had been cut off. He must have been calling from his cell and was not in a good coverage area.

Taylour pushed the button to call him back, but was unable to get through as all circuits were busy. She put the phone down and pulled out of her spot.

She heard the screeching of brakes, and then felt a small bump. Taylour put her car back into Park, and then got out. A 17-year old kid got out of his Mercedes Benz C Class and ran to Taylour.

"Ma'am, are you OK? Sorry 'bout that."

Taylour pursed her lips together and crossed her arms. "I'm fine."

They surveyed the damage, which luckily was not too extensive. Her bumper sustained a large gash that had scraped the paint off, about nine inches long, and his front headlight and bumper had been pushed out of alignment. Since the damage was slight and the two cars were still drivable, they exchanged contact information, including their insurance coverage, and then drove off.

Only after Taylour was back on Hwy 6 headed back to Marlinsville did she notice that Philip had tried to call again. She dialed his number again, and this time it rang.

Philip answered. "Taylour, where have you been?! I've been trying to reach you for the last twenty minutes!"

"What do you mean? What's going on?"

"There's been a shooting!"

Her mouth fell open. "Oh, no!"

The Fallen Body

"It was your foreign friend, whose name is Roman Danshov! He shot the sheriff, apparently after being pulled over by him."

Taylour's hand flew to her chest. "I-Is he OK? That poor man!"

"It is still too early to say, but he was taken to Hillcrest Baptist Medical Center in Waco. The latest I heard is that he was still in surgery, but that was over an hour ago."

"How do they know that it was Roman?"

"Security footage from the camera in the sheriff's patrol car. They've issued a statewide BOLO and have even set up roadblocks on Hwy 6 at both ends and just outside of both Chilton and Kosse on Hwy 7."

Taylour knew that there were several other smaller roads leading out of Marlinsville, but she was counting on him not knowing the area very well. Her face turned ashen. "What if he hasn't left Marlinsville?"

A pause, and then, "I've tried to reach Spencer, but there's no answer on his cell phone, nor on your land line. Is he at home?"

Taylour could not speak as felt her hands and arms shaking. "Philip, where are you? You need to get to my house as soon as you can. I left Spencer alone!"

Images of the photos of the dead body that she had received from the private investigator flashed through her mind.

"I am just outside of Chilton with Sarah."

"You have Sarah with you?" Taylour felt sick and was about to pull over, but she managed to choke down her fear.

"She insisted on coming along. She feels responsible, somehow, and I don't want her out of my sight until this creep is caught and behind bars."

The Fallen Body

Taylour thought quickly. "Then let's meet at the courthouse and go together. I-I'm terrified that Roman may have done harm to Spencer." She gripped the steering wheel until her knuckles were white.

"Sounds good, I'll see about getting some backup. We'll see you in fifteen." Click.

Taylour threw her phone down on the passenger seat and pushed on the accelerator. She whipped around several slow moving cars, honking her horn as she went. She sped past the checkpoint, which got the attention of one of the highway patrolman. She cringed as she saw the flashing blue and red neon lights in her rearview mirror, but she sped on. She was still five minutes from the courthouse.

As she entered Marlinsville, she prayed that nothing happened to Spencer.

Taylour saw Philip's silver SUV ahead already at the courthouse and screeched to a halt next to it. The state highway patrol car whipped to a stop right behind her. She jumped from the car with her hands up as the officer pushed open his door and drew his weapon.

"I'm unarmed!" she yelled, and then stopped her progress towards him so that he would not view her as a threat.

At that moment, Philip leapt from his SUV and whipped out his Texas Rangers badge.

Once the deputy realized that he was not going to be ambushed, he lowered his weapon and motioned for Philip.

"Philip, is that you?" he asked.

Philip, who recognized the voice of his brother, Tom Davidson, acknowledged that it was him.

The Fallen Body

The two of them embraced, and then Philip explained the situation. Tom listened intently, and then talked into his radio for a few minutes.

Taylour hovered nearby, impatiently shuffling back and forth, so Philip grabbed a blanket from the back of his vehicle and wrapped it around her. Sarah stepped out of the SUV and huddled with Taylour under the warm covering.

Tom finally spoke to the group. "I've made a call to get some backup, but it may take a bit of time."

"Officer, we don't have time!" Taylour blurted out. "What if Spencer is in danger?"

"I understand your concern, but we can't just burst upon the scene, especially if the shooter is already there."

"But we have to do something! We can't just stand here."

Philip went to Taylour. "Look, I know that this is hard, but we need to let the authorities take care of this."

Grunting her displeasure, she grabbed the blanket tighter and continued to fidget.

If anything happens to Spencer, so help me, I'll take him down myself.

Chapter 52

"Who are you?" Spencer asked, and then he recognized the man who pushed his way through, a gun pointing directly at Spencer's chest. His legs started to tremble.

"Where is she?"

Spencer threw his hands up and backed away. "H-Hey, man, I don't w-want any trouble."

"Where is she?!"

"W-Who?"

Roman pointed the gun at Spencer's head, right between the eyes. "You know who. Your Auntie Taylour."

"S-She's not here."

Roman lowered the gun, pointed it between Spencer's feet. He fired one round into the wooden floor, and then raised it back up to where it had been just seconds before.

"*Where* is she? I am not going to ask you again."

"Geez, man! You don't have to shoot me! I'll tell you what you want to know."

The Fallen Body

Roman waited. When Spencer didn't continue, Roman made little circles with his hands to get Spencer to keep talking.

"Oh, well, uh, I'm not sure exactly where Taylour is right now. She went Christmas shopping in Waco."

Roman let out a huge sigh, and then motioned with the gun for Spencer to sit down.

Just then, Spencer's cell phone vibrated. Roman grabbed the device from the coffee table and thrust it at Spencer. Without giving him the phone, Roman asked, "Who is this?"

Spencer peered at the number. "That's Philip Davidson, Texas Ranger."

"Why would he be calling you?" When Spencer hesitated, Roman pointed again with the gun.

"I-I dunno! Maybe he is tryin' to find my aunt Taylour." The phone stopped buzzing.

"What has been his involvement with your aunt?"

"Whadda y' mean? Are they dating?" Spencer shook his head and gave a nervous chuckle. "I mean, they like each other and all, but they aren't dating."

Roman clenched his jaw and gritted his teeth. "I did not ask if they were *dating!* What is their professional relationship?"

"Ah, well, they are working together to, ah, find— Hey, would you like something to drink? I mean, we have some cold sodas in the fridge, if you want, I can go get y' one?" Spencer raised his eyebrows in expectation.

This kid is a lunatic! "No, I do not want anything except to know where your aunt is keeping Ms. Baines."

Spencer started rapidly blinking. "Ah, well, if that is what you are looking for, why didn't y' say that sooner. I am, after all, my aunt's office manager. Well, sorta, the office manager. She hasn't started paying me much since I got the job. What I meant to say, is that I might be able to help you out with that."

"You know where Ms. Baines is being held?"

"Well, uh, I didn't say that exactly. But, I might be able to find out where they, I mean, where she is."

Roman' lips curled up into a sneer. "The sooner you tell me, the sooner I will let you go."

Spencer stood up and gave a hesitating nod. He ran his fingers through his hair and shuffled his feet. "Uh, it's not here. Where she's at, I mean. The evidence that you need is not here. It's gonna be at the office."

"Then, let us go get that *evidence*. Now!"

He motioned with the gun to Spencer for him to exit out the front door. They hiked down the driveway to where Roman had hid the Yukon.

"You are driving," Roman said, motioning to Spencer to get in the driver's seat. Roman then crossed in front of the vehicle and got in next to Spencer. He tossed Spencer the keys onto the seat next to him, still training his gun at his chest. "No sudden movements, no calling out for help, or I will shoot you. Understand?"

Spencer took the keys and fumbled to put them in the ignition. "I-I understand."

It was getting dark, so Spencer searched for the headlights to turn them on. When he finally found them, he set them on high beam, and then he pulled out and onto the road. He navigated slowly, taking the turns cautiously, his hands gripping the steering wheel tight enough to make them hurt.

They passed several cars going the opposite direction, but Spencer didn't take off the high beam. As they proceeded towards town, they got several honks from those passing vehicles. After the third honk, Roman sat up in his seat and peered over the dashboard.

The Fallen Body

"You have the bright lights on, you idiot!"

"I don't know how to turn them off! This isn't my car."

Roman reached in front of Spencer, but he couldn't reach with his seat belt holding him back, so he pushed the button to release it. It slid back into place, the metal part of the clip clanking against the interior

As Roman reached in front of Spencer again, Spencer glanced out of the corner of his eye and saw that Roman was no longer restrained, so he searched for the nearest big tree or other obstacle.

Without warning, Spencer swerved to the left, which threw Roman back against the passenger door. Smack! Roman' head hit the window, shattering it to pieces. He dropped the gun on the floorboard.

Spencer straightened the car back into the correct lane and slammed on the brakes, the screeching of rubber on the pavement leaving marks from all four tires. Roman, who was slightly dazed at that point, slammed into the dashboard, effectively knocking the air out of him.

Spencer quickly pushed the release button on his seat belt, and then lunged for the gun. His hands slapped frantically around until they came in contact with the cold steel. Glancing at Roman, who was unconscious, Spencer grabbed the gun, turned the car off, grabbed the keys, and then leapt out of the vehicle.

He had stopped the Yukon on a blind curve, the headlights illuminating the road in front of the SUV. Spencer shook his head to clear the cobwebs and gave silent thanks to the restraint system that saved him from serious injury.

Not seeing any movement coming from the darkened interior, he then decided to investigate. Spencer cast an eerie shadow as he crossed in front of the lights, temporarily blinding him. He backed up from the car and pointed the weapon out in front of him. The passenger door was already open, the seat empty.

He turned around and heard thrashing through the underbrush, so he aimed the gun and fired. Bam! Bam! Bam! He blindly unloaded the magazine towards the sound, pulling the trigger again and again. The clicks of the hammer against an empty chamber finally jolted him from his trance, and he lowered the gun.

There was no moonlight, just the lights from the vehicle, and then those shut off. Spencer ran back to the driver's side and jumped into the Yukon. He turned the car on, put it into gear, and then pressed down on the accelerator. He headed towards Marlinsville to get help.

He spotted a highway patrol car heading towards him going in the opposite direction, so he flashed his lights and honked his horn. After getting the patrol car's attention, he pulled over to the side of the road and slowly got out of the car.

When the officer pulled up behind the vehicle, he recognized the black Yukon from the BOLO. He stopped his car and reached for his gun. He pushed his door open and used it as a shield, his gun drawn on the person stumbling towards him.

"Drop the gun!" He yelled.

"My name is Spencer Dixxon! I need help!"

"Drop the gun, Spencer, and no one will get hurt!"

Realizing that he still had the gun clutched in his hand, he slowly leaned down and placed it on the ground. He raised both hands high in the air and allowed the officer to frisk him. The officer grabbed his handcuffs and put them on Spencer, who appeared dazed, the adrenaline draining from his body.

The Fallen Body

The officer reported in on his shoulder radio, and then motioned for Spencer to sit on the ground. After getting word from his dispatcher, he uncuffed Spencer and guided him to his patrol car, where he placed him gently in the passenger seat.

After a few moments, a caravan of highway patrol vehicles pulled up, their flashing lights casting eerie shadows on the trees.

Taylour pulled up in her car and jumped out. She ran towards Spencer and opened the door.

He stepped out and she gave him a huge squeeze. "Are you OK?"

Spencer, still a bit woozy, gave his aunt a big smile. "Hey, I think I earned my raise today!"

The Fallen Body

Chapter 53

Spencer was examined by an EMT and released. He told his story to a gathering of state patrolmen and patrolwomen, and a few of them were promptly dispatched with search dogs to investigate Roman' disappearance. Seeing that he was exhausted, Taylour gathered him up into her car and took him home to get some sleep.

Because Roman was still on the loose, Philip felt it necessary to go with them, so both he and Sarah followed Taylour and Spencer home.

After Taylour tucked Spencer in upstairs, she came downstairs and sniffed the air. The aroma of greasy bacon and buttermilk pancakes filled the kitchen where Sarah was overseeing the food production. Philip had already pulled plates and silverware out and was seated at the table, waiting.

He stood up as Taylour entered. "I take it that Spencer is safe in bed?"

"Yes, but I hope he doesn't smell this delicious food and want some. He needs his sleep."

The Fallen Body

Taylour and Philip both sat down and looked at each other. They both had so much to talk about, but every attempt to start a meaningful conversation fell flat.

"I heard that the sheriff made it out of surgery OK," Philip said.

"That's great!" Sarah said, and Taylour nodded her agreement as she downed a glass of orange juice.

"I was very worried about him," Taylour added. Silence filled the void as they both watched Sarah flip the pancakes. She was humming to herself, totally oblivious to the tension in the room.

"Spencer sure was brave today, by his telling," Taylour started. "To have a gun pointed at you and then to swerve. That took courage."

"Or he was incredibly lucky. The gun could have gone off, the swerve might not have been enough, or he might have turned the Yukon on its side."

"That's true." Taylour placed her hands in her lap and stared at them intently, not wanting to look at Philip directly. More silence.

Philip made a gun with his right hand and pointed to his left shoulder. "Sheriff got shot right here. Two bullets, and a third grazed the outside of his arm."

"That's nice." Taylour turned to Sarah. "Sarah, is there anything that I can do to help?"

"No, I've got everything under control here."

"Are you sure?"

"Yep, almost done."

Sarah took the last of the pancakes off the griddle and placed them on the table. She then brought the plate of bacon over and placed it next to the syrup.

Glancing at both of them, Sarah put out her hands for them to clasp, and then she said grace.

The Fallen Body

Before Sarah finished, Taylour peeked her eyes at the front door, half expecting someone to come bursting through them, but there was nothing this time.

"Amen!" Philip said, a bit too forcefully, and then he attacked the stack of pancakes with his fork. After getting three, he passed the plate and reached for the syrup.

Sarah glanced at Taylour and saw something that she had dreaded all along. Taylour had a beaming expression, her cheeks glowing as she shook her head at Philip's antics. Sarah knew that look and felt her stomach harden. She swiped the tears from her cheeks and shoved the hair out of her eyes.

"Sarah, are you OK?" asked Taylour. Her concerned look at Sarah caused Sarah to laugh clumsily.

"I'm fine, it's just been an exhausting day."

Taylour went to say something else, but decided not to.

The three of them ate in silence.

A metallic ring came from the phone on the wall, so Taylour jumped up to answer it.

"Hello, this is Taylour."

Sarah and Philip heard talking on the other end as Taylour listened for several minutes without interrupting.

"Thank you!" She slowly cradled the receiver back onto the wall.

"What?" Philip and Sarah said in unison.

"They found Roman." Relief washed over her face. "He appears to have hit his head on a rock while stumbling around. They found his dead body and wanted us to know."

Just then, Philip's phone sounded and he flipped it open. He stood up and excused himself from the room. He came back moments later with a shocked look on his face.

The Fallen Body

Their two faces gazed expectantly up at him. "I've just been given a new assignment."

Taylour's eyes fell. She didn't want him to leave, not yet. Sarah gave Taylour a sidelong look and sighed.

Philip, not quite understanding the two reactions that he got, blurted out, "I've been asked to stay on as the sheriff here in Marlinsville."

Taylour jumped up and threw her arms around him. "I didn't want you to go, not yet."

They embraced, and then, as if on cue, they separated and sheepishly looked at Sarah.

Sarah pushed her jealousy aside and stood up. She reached out to both of them and hugged them tight, never wanting to let go.

The Fallen Body

Chapter 54

After her confrontation with Neal, Sarah wandered around downtown Dallas, stopping every now and then to smell the rich aromas that wafted in the air. She found a small cafe that was still open, sat down, and had a cup of coffee. She nursed the drink in her hands, using the cup to keep her hands warm in the brisk autumn air. She looked at her phone, saw what time it was, and then decided to wait a little longer.

Finally, after fifteen more minutes, she paid her bill and made her way back to The Tower Residences. As she approached the building, she saw the flashing neon blue and red lights of several police cars. Trying to get a better view, she drew closer. Nudging people aside, she leaned up against the police tape. She stifled a gasp. Her husband's body had fallen on her rental car.

She fled from the crowd that had gathered to watch, almost tripping from the speed of her departure, as tears streamed down her face, stinging her flushed cheeks with guilt.

* * *

Taylour hoped that even though it was the day before Christmas that it was not going to be too busy at the office as she had invited Philip and Sarah to brunch the next day. With everything that had been going on, the decorations, including a Christmas tree, were not completely hung, so she tasked Spencer with finding a tree to put in their front room.

Sarah had told her that she wanted to come by and drop off the final check that she owed her for her services. She said that it would include a nice bonus for a job well done. The funds were badly needed to fill an ever-depleting bank account.

As Taylour sat at her desk, a nagging thought came to mind. Where were the photos of Roman, and what had she done with the package that the private investigator had sent? She rifled through the stack on her desk and found the envelope.

Ow! Her hand jerked back as she got a paper cut. A drop of blood formed on the end of her finger, so instinctively she stuck it in her mouth to moisten it. She scrunched her face from the metallic taste, and then she searched in her drawer for a bandage. Once she stopped the bleeding, Taylour continued her search, more carefully this time.

She felt herself tense up as she flipped through the photos that she had already seen. There was a group of stock photos that appeared to be from a cocktail party for some charitable event in New York. She stopped on a picture of Roman, who had a beautiful, platinum blonde clinging to one arm.

She picked up the photo to take a closer look, and then gasped. The photo fell back onto the desk, and then Taylour scrambled through her desk to find a magnifying glass. She found it buried under some yellow Post-it notes and snatched it up. As she focused the lens on the blonde, the unmistakable face of Sarah Baines stared back at her.

Clang! Clang! The bell on the front door announced a visitor. Taylour jumped from her chair and went out into the hallway. Sarah came towards her with her purse slung on one arm. She reached inside and pulled something out.

"Here's the check I promised." Sarah smiled, and then extended the check to Taylour.

At first, Taylour just stared at it. How does Sarah know the man who allegedly killed her husband? Was this a chance encounter? Or something more sinister?

Standing at the entrance to her private office, she cleared her throat, wiped her hands on her shirt, and then took the check. She held it behind her, not wanting to look at it. Do I invite her in to sit? No! I can't let her see the photo!

Sarah tilted her head and squinted her eyes at Taylour. "Is everything OK?"

"Yes! I mean, no, uh." Taylour stalled for time so that her mind could process what she had just discovered. "Sorry, I was a bit surprised to see you so early this morning."

Sarah relaxed a bit and said, "I thought I told you I was going to come by. I guess I didn't say exactly when." She shifted her weight on her feet, which Taylour immediately noticed.

"Oh, I'm sorry! I didn't invite you in." She extended her hand to the kitchen instead of towards her office, which caused Sarah to tilt her head slightly in confusion. Taylour grabbed Sarah by the arm and showed her to a chair. Sarah hesitated.

"Wouldn't we be more comfortable in your office?"

"Uh, my office is a mess right now." Taylour realized that she was still standing, holding the check. "Sorry, let me go put this, er, check down before I lose it. Excuse me for just a moment."

The Fallen Body

Taylour whirled around and went back into her office. She quickly dropped the check next to her computer monitor, and then turned to her desk to gather up the contents of the package. As she shuffled the photos and papers together, she glanced up.

She was startled to see Sarah standing in the doorway. Instinctively, she looked down at the photos and papers, trying to file them away.

"What are those?" Sarah saw the top photo and snatched it from the pile. Taylour watched her reaction as Sarah examined the photo. Curiosity, recognition, fear, and then calm.

"You are still my lawyer, correct?"

"How could you do this? I trusted you. We all trusted you!"

Sarah's eyes went cold, and her voice went frosty. "My husband was cheating on me! On *me*!"

"So you intended to kill him all along, didn't you? When you went into his apartment, you had a gun, and you shot him."

Sarah sat down and covered her eyes. "I didn't shoot him." She shook her head. "I-I didn't have the nerve."

Taylour was puzzled. "So, how did your gun get to Roman? The forensic evidence clearly indicated that your gun was the murder weapon."

Sarah sighed. She stared at the wall for what seemed like an eternity, and then tried to hold Taylour's gaze, but failed. "I had a backup plan. I arranged for Roman to be there, and if I gave a prearranged signal, then he would... he would—"

"The prearranged signal was you dumping the gun in the trash can, right?"

Sarah nodded.

The Fallen Body

"So Roman took the gun, went to Neal's apartment, and shot him?" Taylour thought for a moment, and then asked, "But you didn't go to the doorman to ask which apartment Neal was in, right? If you didn't know the number, how did Roman know?"

"We both knew the number."

"So why was Roman here, in Marlinsville?"

Sarah pointed to the package. "Because of that. I met Roman at that party, and we hit it off. But he never really trusted me, so I think he came looking for me. Maybe he thought I would tell the truth about his involvement.

Taylour threw her hands out in exasperation. "But you were so convincing! The crying, the vulnerability that you showed, the bond that we had! Or thought that we had."

"You forget. I am an actress, deserving of an Academy Award for my performance, if I do say so."

"So none of it was real?"

Sarah paused. "I wouldn't say that. Maybe parts were real, like how I felt doing this to my parents, which helped to fuel the grief." Sarah finally managed to look at Taylour. "Or how we seemed to connect."

"Why didn't you just tell me the truth in the beginning? I might have approached the case a bit differently, but I still would have defended you."

Sarah fidgeted in her chair. "I wanted to keep it hidden. I didn't think that I could trust you, really trust you."

Taylour slapped her desk with her hands. Why did this always happen? Her clients hire her because they need real help, but then they are almost incapable of telling the truth. Is it shame? Guilt? She shook her head.

The Fallen Body

Something was still bothering Taylour. "Who is Dmitri? Philip thought that he was the one that hired Roman to come looking for you."

"Dmitri is a nobody. He is someone that is about to go to prison for the rest of his life. Or he was, until my husband's client disappeared. Now, I'm not so sure."

"But why go after me?"

"That's the way he works. He intimidates people. Since he couldn't find me, he thought he could intimidate you so that through you, he gets to me. He was letting me know that he was watching."

"You knew all this, and yet you said nothing?"

Sarah stared at the stapler on Taylour's desk.

Taylour spoke in a soft whisper. "Sarah, despite the feelings of betrayal that I have for you right now, I am still your lawyer. But..." She took a deep breath and let it out with a heavy sigh. "I cannot be your friend."

A heavy cloud hung in the air, the stillness palpable. They both sat, frozen, until Sarah broke the silence.

"I-I understand." She slowly rose from her seat and exited. Taylour heard her footfalls recede down the hall, and then the tinny sound of the bell as the door opened, and then closed.

Taylour still did not move, her mind trying desperately to process what just happened. She wiped the moisture from her cheeks and asked herself for the thousandth time, is it all worth it?

Chapter 55

Taylour, Philip, and Spencer celebrated Christmas brunch together. They exchanged the gifts that they had bought each other, and then laughed and sang carols at the top of their lungs.

In the middle of the festivities, Taylour excused herself when she heard a knock on the door.

She opened it slightly, said thank you, and then yelled, "Spencer, I think it's for you."

Spencer came up behind Taylour, who was blocking his view. She stepped aside to reveal a golden retriever puppy playing with a red bow wrapped around its neck.

A squeal of delight, and then Spencer scooped up his present. He nuzzled him and the mass of hair stuck out its tongue and licked Spencer's neck playfully. He hugged Taylour fiercely, and then went to get his new puppy some food and water.

Taylour got melancholy when Philip said that he needed to leave. He said that his father and brother were expecting him for dinner.

She walked Philip out to his car and lingered on the porch as he drove off. As she waved good-bye, she sighed happily. Life, even with all of its challenges, was pretty

The Fallen Body

good right now. Having Spencer around was good for her, he was someone that she could take care of, and he seemed to like it here.

But, most of all, she wondered about Philip. Until he had come along, she hadn't been that happy. Now she felt giddy, and life suddenly made sense with him.

In the end, after all the struggles to keep her law practice open, it was worth it. Taylour received satisfaction knowing that her clients turned to her for help because they had no other option. She might not have a fancy office in a prestigious law firm, but deep down she longed for the satisfaction that only came from helping those in her community, from her neighbor and his estate questions, to the mysterious millionairess with a deadly secret. Taylour knew that working for a big-name law office would not bring her the same level of happiness.

That is why Taylour stayed in Marlinsville. Because she belonged.

Stone Patrick is a pseudonym for Taylor Stonely, who has a day job working for a financial services company. He received a BS degree from Brigham Young in 1991 and an MBA degree from the University of Phoenix in 2002. He currently resides in north Texas with his wife and four children. While he is a frequent blogger on his website, www.taylorsbookpub.com, "The Fallen Body" is his debut suspense novel.

Made in the USA
Charleston, SC
13 December 2013